NOT ANOTHER FAMILY WEDDING

CHIN-WILLIAMS, BOOK 1

JACKIE LAU

First edition: September 2018
ISBN: 978-1-989610-05-3

Editor: Latoya C. Smith, LCS Literary Services

Cover Design: Flirtation Designs

Cover photograph: Shutterstock

[1]

ONCE UPON A TIME, in the not-so-idyllic small town of Mosquito Bay, Ontario, Natalie Chin-Williams used to play wedding with her little sister.

At sixteen, Natalie would roll her eyes if her mother asked her to put away dishes, but if her five-year-old sister, Rebecca, asked her to play wedding, she would always oblige, even though she'd done it dozens of times before. Usually Rebecca wanted to marry her big stuffed gorilla, the one Dad had won—a total fluke—at the fair, but occasionally she wanted to marry one of her dolls or Natalie's old teddy bear, Fuzzy Wuzzy.

Now, twenty years later, over steaming cups of hot chocolate with whipped cream, Rebecca was talking about her real wedding. To a man, not a stuffed animal.

"May twentieth," Rebecca said. "That's our wedding date."

Natalie nodded. That was reasonable. More than a year to plan the wedding. Rebecca had revealed she was engaged at Christmas, and Natalie had secretly hoped for a long engagement. At least a year. Maybe two.

Apparently, she was getting her Christmas wish.

It was the middle of February now. Winterlude in Ottawa.

Rebecca had come up from Toronto to visit Natalie for the weekend, and after looking at the ice sculptures in Confederation Park, they'd skated along the Rideau Canal to Bank Street, where they were now sitting in a coffee shop.

Natalie raised her cup of hot chocolate to her lips and got a mouthful of whipped cream with a hint of chocolate.

"May twentieth of this year," Rebecca clarified.

Natalie choked on her next sip of hot chocolate. "You're getting married in three months?" she croaked.

"That's right."

It had been silly to assume her sister meant next year, but that had seemed like the sensible assumption. "How are you going to plan a wedding in such a short time? Don't the venues in Toronto fill up a year in advance?"

Rebecca sat forward in her seat. "We're getting married in Mosquito Bay."

Oh. How lovely.

Their hometown was two and a half hours west of Toronto on Lake Huron. Natalie had been desperate to escape when she finished high school.

"You're going to get married at the United Church and have the reception at the community center?" she asked. That was pretty much the only option in the tiny town.

Rebecca frowned. "You're unhappy, aren't you? You don't think I should get married there? Wait—or do you not like Elliot?"

Natalie liked Elliot just fine, but she'd only met him twice. Once at Thanksgiving, and once at Christmas. He and Rebecca had been together for barely six months, and it seemed a little fast, that was all. Hence her hope for a long engagement.

More hot chocolate. "I just want you to be sure. You haven't been together long, and you're only twenty-five." *I can't wrap my head around this. I keep thinking of the day Mom brought you home from the hospital.*

Natalie might call herself cranky and unsentimental, and she wasn't really the nurturing type, but where her sister was concerned, it was different. Twenty-five years ago, Rebecca had come home from the hospital swaddled in a pink blanket, and Natalie had loved her from the very beginning, had always taken special care of her. She'd dried her sister's tears, protected her from the trolls in her closet…and officiated seventeen wedding ceremonies for Rebecca and Misty Gorilly.

"I'm sure," Rebecca said eagerly. "I just *know*."

Dammit, she seemed so happy. Natalie wouldn't voice any more doubts, even though the last friend who'd told her that she "just knew" had gotten divorced two years later. But Rebecca had seemed in particularly good spirits since she'd met Elliot, and it wasn't like they'd been together only a month or two.

"Will you be my bridesmaid?" Rebecca asked. "Please?" She licked her whipped cream, which she'd sprinkled with cinnamon and chocolate shavings.

Natalie smiled. "Of course."

Rebecca stood up and wrapped her arms around Natalie, who returned the hug.

It was official. Her little sister, who was eleven years younger than her, would beat her to the altar. Although Natalie would act like it didn't bother her, if she was honest, she was a tiny bit jealous. She rarely admitted it—even to herself—but she would like to get married someday. It seemed unlikely, though, given her long history of failed relationships, as well as the fact that the men she dated always had a very different view of her future than she did.

Still, life wasn't bad. She'd recently gotten tenure and become an associate professor. As a climatologist, she spent her days discovering over and over again that the world was fucked.

Cheerful stuff.

"Are you inviting Grandma and Uncle Dennis?" Natalie asked.

"Why wouldn't I?" Rebecca sat back down. "They're family. I'm inviting everyone."

"They're horrible human beings."

And now that Natalie thought of her extended family being in one room together, she had a sinking feeling.

It was going to be a disaster.

Just like every other wedding in her family.

It had started with her parents' wedding nearly forty years ago. Her mother's parents hadn't come because they were unhappy she was marrying a Chinese man. Her father's parents hadn't come because they were unhappy he was marrying a white woman. Of their four siblings, only Aunt Louisa had made an appearance.

So that was a happy occasion. It had been a small affair in Toronto, attended mostly by friends.

Then there was Uncle Carey's wedding, twenty years ago, at which Rebecca had been a flower girl. Grandma and Grandpa had approved of his wife-to-be, so they'd attended. But Grandma got into a huge fight with Uncle Carey's new mother-in-law, both of them very drunk, and one of the bridesmaids was caught having sex—with someone other than her fiancé—in the washroom.

But that wasn't the worst part.

No, the worst part was the food poisoning.

Rebecca had ended up in the hospital because she'd been severely dehydrated. Natalie, the only person in her immediate family who wasn't puking, had kept her company. Seeing her sister hooked up to an IV to receive fluids and salts—that was rough. Natalie had held her hand and read her stories and tried not to show how freaked out she was. Fortunately, Rebecca recovered quickly, but after that incident, she lost interest in weddings. She no longer wanted to marry Misty Gorilly or Fuzzy Wuzzy in elaborate ceremonies in her bedroom.

Lastly, there was Seth's wedding. Natalie chuckled as she

remembered the Wedding Cake Incident, and then shuddered as she remembered everything else. That was more than nine years ago now, and she couldn't believe she was old enough to have a brother who'd been married for that long.

The one person who'd been blessed with good luck on her wedding day was Aunt Louisa. Weddings two and three had gone fine, too, but she'd recently divorced her third husband.

Hopefully Rebecca's marriage to Elliot would be happy. However, it was probably too much to ask that the wedding itself would be free of drama. Natalie wanted everything to go perfectly for her sister's big day, but that seemed unlikely.

She sipped her hot chocolate and wished it was full of booze. Bailey's, amaretto, whiskey…she wasn't picky.

"It'll be fine," Rebecca said. "I'm marrying a white guy, so Grandma and Uncle Dennis will probably be reasonably well behaved. I can't just not invite them."

Yeah, you can, and everyone would understand. Unfortunately, Natalie knew there was no changing her sister's mind.

"I know you're uncomfortable because Elliot and I haven't been together very long. But neither had Mom and Dad when they got married, and they're still together."

Yes, despite all the people who'd been against their marriage, Mom and Dad would celebrate their fortieth anniversary in September. Natalie made a mental note to plan something for that.

"Let me show you some of the bridesmaid dresses I've been looking at." Rebecca pulled out her phone.

Natalie blew out a breath and turned her chair so she could look at the screen. She provided opinions on the dresses her sister showed her, but her mind was elsewhere.

Although she'd mostly accepted her single status, she wished she had a boyfriend to bring to Rebecca's wedding. Someone to support her through what would inevitably be a difficult day. Plus, if she had a boyfriend, she wouldn't get as many comments about how her biological clock was ticking and she was so old to be unmarried. Now that she was thirty-six, she was getting more and more of those. Why did people feel the need to ask such rude and intrusive questions?

Natalie didn't have much chance of getting a boyfriend before Rebecca's wedding, and she wasn't crazy enough to ask someone to be her fake boyfriend. Perhaps she could find a date, though.

But who?

Well, in case there was food poisoning, it might be helpful to have a doctor on hand.

Connor. That's what she would do. She'd ask Connor.

She smiled at the thought of her friend.

Connor Douglas followed his sister into the playroom. Brightly colored toys of all sorts were scattered across the floor, and it looked like a tornado had hit. However, his three-year-old niece, Ariana, was sitting at a table, quietly scribbling.

Quiet. And sitting.

This might qualify as a miracle.

He and Mallory stood near the doorway for a minute, enjoying the silence.

Ariana scrunched up her face, as though trying to figure out a difficult problem—it was pretty cute. She stood up and walked to the back wall. Connor wondered what she would do there.

Mallory was already hurrying across the room. She swept Ariana off the floor just before Ariana's red crayon touched the wall.

Ah. So that's what was going on.

"What did I tell you about crayons?" Mallory demanded, setting her daughter down at the child-sized table.

Ariana rolled her eyes. "Crayons are only for paper. Not for walls." She spoke as though she were a teenager with the weight of the world on her shoulders.

"Then why were you going to draw on the wall?"

"Because Uncle Connor is coming, so it's a special occasion!"

He suppressed a smile.

"Ariana," Mallory said. "You cannot draw on the wall, *even if it's a special occasion.*"

"Last weekend you let me have two cookies because it was Daddy's birthday."

"An extra cookie is not the same as drawing on the wall."

"Why not?" Ariana crossed her arms over her chest.

Connor stepped forward and knelt in front of his niece. "Why don't we play zookeeper?"

"Uncle Connor! You're here!" She threw her arms around his neck, and he smiled as he hugged her back. "Except now you're Hippo Connor. What kind of sounds do hippos make?"

"I don't know."

"You're an adult. You're supposed to know everything."

He growled low in his throat. "Maybe that's what they do? To warn the other hippos when the lions are coming?"

"But the lions are in their own cages! You're silly, Hippo Connor." Ariana scampered out of the room, calling out, "I need to get my fish."

"It's a new part of playing zookeeper," Mallory explained. "She saw someone feeding fish to penguins on TV, and now she wants to feed her bath toy fish to the animals in her zoo. Whether they're hippos, lions, or panda bears." She headed to the front door. "See you in a few hours. Have fun!"

Connor got down on his hands and knees so he'd look more like a hippo. When Ariana ran back into the playroom, bucket of fish in hand, she jumped on his back.

"Let's go, Hippo Connor! Time to visit the elephants!"

Two hours later, in addition to a hippo, Connor had been a tiger, a flamingo, an elephant, a peacock, and a stegosaurus, all of which had been fed plastic rainbow-colored fish. Ariana had informed him that stegosaurus had a walnut for a brain, and then she'd gone to the living room, dumped a bowl of nuts on the floor, and ran around the house screaming for five minutes.

He still hadn't figured out what that was about.

Next, they'd played hide-and-seek, and that had been fun, but after three hours with Ariana, he was ready to go home and watch Netflix in peace. Maybe drink a beer.

Was his niece a difficult child? He wasn't sure. Perhaps she was a pretty normal three-year-old, but he still didn't know how Mallory managed.

When his sister arrived home, he was crawling around the playroom with a toilet paper roll taped to his forehead.

Mallory laughed. "What happened to Uncle Connor?"

"He's a unicorn now!" Ariana announced proudly. "Mommy, where's the glitter? Unicorns should have glitter."

"No glitter."

"But it's a special occasion!"

"I said *no.*"

Ariana promptly threw a tantrum, but five minutes later, all was forgotten and she was crawling around the room with her own unicorn horn.

When Connor was at the door, ready to say goodbye to his sister, he noticed the dark circles under her eyes and the enormous brown stain on her shirt.

"What's that?" he asked, pointing at the stain.

Mallory laughed without humor. "I don't know. I didn't even see it until I'd gotten to the coffee shop."

God, she looks tired.

"You need a break," he said. "A weekend away."

She shook her head. "Mom and Dad won't look after Ariana for that long."

"But I will. Why don't you do something for your wedding anniversary? I can take her for two nights. You could go to Montreal or Quebec City. Or a spa in Vermont." Did they have fancy spas in Vermont? He assumed they did.

She hugged him and said he was the best brother in the world.

He loved his niece, but he'd never looked after a child for a whole weekend before. The idea was rather overwhelming.

He had a feeling he was going to regret this.

[2]

A WEEK LATER, Natalie met Connor at their favorite brew pub.

"That has to be clogging your arteries like crazy," she said as he picked up a gravy-covered fry with cheese curds.

"Luckily I have this to balance it out." He raised his pint of pilsner.

She chuckled and looked down at her plate. A burger and salad. It seemed healthy in comparison to his large serving of poutine.

But Connor was a large guy. He needed a lot more calories to keep him going than she did. He was over six feet tall, and although he didn't have perfectly sculpted muscles, he was… solid. That's how she thought of him, both physically and in other ways. He was dependable.

They had been friends since they were chemistry lab partners in their first year at the University of Toronto. That was seventeen years ago now; she couldn't believe it had been so long. They'd kept in touch when she went out to Vancouver for grad school, and when she got the job at the university in Ottawa, she'd been glad that she would get to hang out with Connor regularly. He'd set up his family medicine practice here since that's where his wife was from and she'd wanted to be near her family.

He wasn't married anymore, though, which was why he could be Natalie's date for the wedding.

"So." He picked up another fry. "You said you had something to ask me?"

Dammit. Why did he have to ask that question just after she'd bitten into her juicy burger? She rarely ate beef—it was terrible for the environment—so this was a luxury for her.

She didn't answer right away. No, she proceeded to enjoy that bite as much as she could.

"A favor," she said at last. "A rather big favor, in fact."

Now that she was about to ask him, she was a little nervous, which was weird—she never felt nervous around Connor. What was the worst that could happen? He'd say no, and she'd have to go to her sister's wedding without a date.

Actually, that was kind of bad. She'd really prefer to have some emotional support for what could end up being a disaster of epic proportions.

That's what friends were for, right?

"My sister," she continued, "set a date for her wedding. She's getting married in May, on the Victoria Day weekend. This year."

"So much for your hope of a long engagement."

"Yeah, so much for that."

"It's amazing that she's old enough to get married. You used to tell me stories about her when we were working on our labs. I guess she would have been seven or eight then."

Natalie had been eager to escape Mosquito Bay for university, but there had been one drawback: she couldn't see her little sister every day. She hadn't really missed her parents or Seth, but she'd missed Rebecca.

"So, what's the favor?" Connor asked.

"I want you to be my date."

"You want *me* to be your *date*?" He coughed a few times, his face turning slightly red.

"You okay?"

He held up a finger and nodded. A moment later, he said, "Sorry about that."

"Was the prospect of being my date so horrifying that it made you choke?"

"Of course not. It was just a surprise. Why do you want a date?"

"Remember how weddings are always a disaster in my family?"

"I remember your stories of Seth's wedding. How your uncle made racist comments, your brother's husband tripped and fell into the wedding cake, your grandparents refused to come because your brother was marrying a man—"

"And not just any man, but a Chinese one. Plus, one guest attacked another with lobster claws, and he had to get stitches. That about covers it."

"A very cheerful affair."

"Indeed, it was." Natalie swiped one of Connor's fries. "But maybe it was better than my uncle's wedding. Half the guests ended up with food poisoning."

His eyes widened.

"So, are you willing to be my date? The wedding's in Mosquito Bay. We'll need to take your car, unless you're happy with the train."

Natalie didn't have a car. She was an environmentalist, after all. She got by just fine in Ottawa without one, and when she went to Toronto, she took the train. When traveling to Mosquito Bay, she either took the train to London, where her dad picked her up, or rented a car.

Connor crossed his arms on the table and leaned forward.

"I'll do it," he said. "As long as you give me something in return."

Oh, God. What was happening? Was Connor going to ask for

sexual favors in exchange for being his date?

No, that was ridiculous. He'd never shown any interest in her in that way. Not when they were university students, not after he was divorced, and certainly not during his marriage. She was just imagining it.

Wasn't she?

"I need you to help me look after my niece," he said.

Right. Connor would *never* want anything like that from her, and that was totally cool. Wasn't like she'd ever had a crush on him. They were just friends.

"Look after your niece," she repeated faintly, trying to clear her head. "Just for an afternoon?"

"I volunteered to watch Ariana for a weekend so my sister and her husband can go away for their anniversary."

"How old is she now?"

"She'll be four next month."

Many women would turn to mush if a guy told them that he'd offered to babysit his niece for a weekend. But not Natalie.

Although, yeah, it was kind of sweet.

"I've looked after her for an afternoon," Connor said. "That's no problem. Even if I have to pretend to be a unicorn with a toilet paper roll affixed to my forehead."

Natalie snickered.

"But I don't know how to entertain her for a whole weekend, and I'm worried about putting her to bed. Apparently, she's not the greatest with bedtime."

"Do you want me to stay at your place all weekend to help?"

The thought of spending so much time with him, both for Rebecca's wedding and to help with Ariana…

What is wrong with you, Natalie?

"No," he said. "Just come over for a few hours on the Friday, help me put her to bed. Then, depending on how that goes, I might need your help on Saturday. You had lots of practice with your sister, so I figure you'll be better at this than me."

"Sure. No problem." That was more than a fair trade, and Natalie liked children.

In small doses.

That was part of the problem with her dating life. The men who liked her always wanted children, and she didn't.

And she refused to compromise on that issue.

She pushed those thoughts aside and looked up at Connor. "Just so you're clear on what you're signing up for, Mosquito Bay is a seven-hour drive from here, depending on how long it takes to get through Toronto, and my family is absolutely nuts. It'll be particularly bad because Rebecca has insisted on inviting Grandma and Uncle Dennis to the wedding, and they are hardly the picture of tolerance and good behavior. Fortunately, the catering company responsible for the food poisoning has gone out of business, so I don't think you have much to worry about there, though I can't make any guarantees."

"And just so *you* know what you're signing up for... My niece is a bit of a handful."

"I can manage." Natalie stuck out her hand. "Pleasure doing business with you, Dr. Douglas."

He shook her hand. "Pleasure doing business with you, too, Professor."

Connor breathed in the crisp air and smiled. It was a lovely winter day, and he and Natalie were cross-country skiing at a park not far from Ottawa, in Quebec. They'd usually ski together a few times a year, and in the warmer months, they'd sometimes go hiking. They both preferred living in the city but also enjoyed escaping urban life and spending time outdoors.

They leisurely made their way along the groomed trails through the woods. The evergreen trees were laden with fluffy snow. In the distance, he heard a bird—maybe a cardinal.

Natalie was ahead of him, in her red snow pants and jacket. He'd last seen her two weeks ago at the pub, where he'd agreed to be her date for her sister's wedding.

Her date.

Once, the idea would have thrilled him. He'd developed quite a crush on her back when they were chemistry lab partners. He'd loved the way she'd wrinkle her nose or twist her mouth in concentration; he'd loved the purple streaks she used to have in her hair. He remembered the first time they'd eaten dinner together—just falafel sandwiches, but he'd enjoyed it so much.

However, she'd gotten a boyfriend a few months after they'd met, and he'd forced himself to get over his crush because he didn't want to have a crush on someone who was in a relationship. It had taken a while, but he'd managed, and they'd become good friends.

He was happy to be her date now—even if she wouldn't help with Ariana, he would have done it—but the idea didn't give him an electric thrill like it would have seventeen years ago.

The sun came out from behind the clouds and filtered through the bare branches and conifers. Up ahead, Natalie came to a stop and tipped her face toward the sun.

"It's so peaceful here," she said.

"It is."

Natalie loved nature and wanted to preserve it for future generations, although whenever she talked about climate change, she always sounded more than a little pessimistic. Disappearing glaciers, growing deserts, species on the brink of extinction, governments refusing to take appropriate action.

She was passionate and a bit prickly. Yes, that was a good description of Natalie.

She started skiing again, continuing along the ten-kilometer trail through the woods, and he followed her.

Later that afternoon, they returned to Natalie's condo and took off their winter gear, and she pulled out a bag of Cheetos, her typical post-skiing and post-hiking snack. She dumped them into a bowl, then picked up a single piece with a pair of chopsticks—this was what she always did, so her hands didn't get messy. She'd been doing it since long before that photo of Oscar Isaac eating Cheetos with chopsticks went viral.

Connor had long known of Natalie's love for Cheetos and had seen her eat them this way many times before. He'd also seen her slightly flushed after a day of exercise, her hair going every which way after being stuck under a toque.

But for some reason, this time was different.

This time, he thought she was rather adorable, and he wanted to pull the chopsticks out of her hand and feed her the orange, cheese-flavored snack food himself. Lick the crumbs off her lips and kiss her.

How odd.

She reached for another Cheeto and frowned. "Why are you looking at me funny?"

Shit. What should he say? "Your hair's a mess, that's all."

He hadn't thought of Natalie this way in well over a decade. She was a friend, nothing more, but now he couldn't help remembering his long-ago crush, how he'd sneak peeks at her as she scribbled in her lab book.

He grabbed a handful of Cheetos, and when he looked at her again, that feeling was gone.

It had been just a fleeting feeling. Surely it meant nothing.

He didn't feel that way again in the following months. Not any of the times they met for beers or went hiking in Gatineau Park. They even talked about going to Gros Morne National Park in Newfoundland together, maybe at the end of August, and the thought of a week-long trip with Natalie didn't make him think of her as anything but a close friend.

There was no repeat of the way he'd felt when she'd popped that Cheeto into her mouth.

Not until the day before Rebecca's wedding in May.

[3]

When Connor and Natalie finally arrived in Mosquito Bay, it was four thirty on the Friday before the Victoria Day long weekend. It had taken them all day to get there. Connor looked around as he drove down the quiet residential streets. So this was where Natalie Chin-Williams was from, this sleepy little town on Lake Huron.

"Why is it called Mosquito Bay?" he asked. "Are there lots of mosquitoes?"

She shrugged. "There are certainly mosquitoes, but no worse than anywhere else in the area. The name's enough to discourage tourists, however. When I was in high school, there was a petition to change it, which led to the most exciting town hall meeting ever."

He was looking at the road, but he imagined Natalie rolling her eyes. "I'm sure it was."

"Oh, yeah. It was *legendary*," she said, before directing him to Maple Grove Lane, number forty-four. "This is the house. My grandma—"

"Which one?"

"The Asian one. She was aghast when my parents bought it

because four is considered an unlucky number. It sounds like the word for death in Chinese."

Connor parked his car on the road since the driveway was full.

This was it. But it wasn't like he was meeting his girlfriend's parents for the first time—something he hadn't done in over ten years, not since Sharon had brought him home when they were in med school. He'd been a nervous wreck then, but he didn't feel so bad now, except that after the long drive, he desperately needed some fresh air.

Meeting his friend's family, though? No big deal.

Yes, Natalie had spent the past hour emphasizing that her family was crazy, but it seemed to be mostly her extended family, and they wouldn't be at the rehearsal tonight. Either way, he could manage.

There were two young men sitting on red Muskoka chairs on the front lawn, each holding a bottle of beer. The man on the left bore a close resemblance to Natalie—that must be her brother, Seth. The Asian man on the right had fair skin and short black hair, and he was slighter in stature than Seth.

Connor and Natalie got out of the car, and the man on the right immediately jumped up and hurried over to them. He enthusiastically pumped Connor's hand up and down. "You must be Natalie's new boyfriend." He had a faint British accent.

"No," Connor said. "We're actually—"

"We're just friends," Natalie said.

The man pulled his hand back and nodded knowingly. "Ah. You're already finishing each other's sentences."

"Simon," Natalie said, "this is Connor. My *friend*."

Simon looked back at Seth. "Dammit. You said Natalie was bringing a boyfriend."

"I did," Seth said mildly. "That's what Mom told me. I was just repeating what I heard."

"Connor's cute," Simon said, leaning toward Natalie. "Maybe

you should change that 'he's just a friend' business. Are you sharing a room at the bed and breakfast?"

"He's staying there by himself," Natalie said. "I'll stay with Mom and Dad."

Simon shook his head. "I'm disappointed in you."

She turned to Connor. "Simon is Seth's husband, in case you hadn't figured that out."

"You're the man who fell on his own wedding cake," Connor said.

"That would be me." Simon sighed dramatically. "I've had to accept that no one will ever forget about the time I did a face-plant into a three-tier chocolate cake."

"Why would they?" Seth asked. "It was a very pretty face-plant. And there's photographic *and* video evidence."

Simon shot him a mock glare that quickly turned into a smile.

Natalie bent over and gave her brother, who was still sitting down, a one-armed hug. "What do you think will happen at Rebecca's wedding?"

"I don't want to consider the possibilities."

"Grandma and Uncle Dennis are still coming, I assume?"

"As far as I know." Seth's face hardened. "Not that I have any intention of going near them." He had a sip of beer. "Simon spent the entire flight speculating about your boyfriend."

"Connor's not my—"

"Yeah. I figured that out the first time you said it."

An older white woman with graying brown hair walked down the flagstone path to the lawn. Natalie's mother, Connor presumed. She looked a little flustered.

"Judy!" Simon said. "Turns out you were wrong. Connor isn't Natalie's boyfriend after all. They're just friends."

Connor could handle Natalie's family, but he had a feeling he'd get rather sick of repeating, "We're just friends."

"Sorry, I must have misheard," Judy said absently before

giving Natalie a hug. "Where's Rebecca? She should be here by now. I think Iris is coming here before the rehearsal, too."

"Iris is our cousin," Natalie explained. "She's a year older than Rebecca."

"You must be Natalie's *not* boyfriend," Judy said, extending her hand.

"Connor." He shook her hand, which was rather cold despite the warm weather. "Pleased to meet you."

"So, Connor," Simon said, shoving his hands in his pockets and rocking back on his heels. "You must have had to miss a day of work to come all the way to Mosquito Bay."

"I would have closed the office for the afternoon before the long weekend anyway. Just gave everyone the day off instead."

"Ah. You're the boss. What do you do?"

"I'm a family physician."

"A doctor." Simon laughed. "Oh my God, Ngin Ngin is going to love this."

Before Connor could ask who Ngin Ngin was, a car pulled up. Natalie smiled as a young woman in a floral-print dress stepped out of the car. They looked just like sisters, though Rebecca didn't look quite as Chinese as Natalie did. Something about the shape of her features and her hair color, which was lighter than Natalie's near-black hair.

"You can all stop worrying," Rebecca said. "The bride is here!" She threw her arms around Natalie. "It's so good to see you!"

Rebecca's fiancé joined them on the lawn, and then everyone was talking at once, and Connor lost track of the conversation. It was nice seeing Natalie with her family. For all she complained about them, she seemed content here. He pictured her as a young girl, skipping rope or playing catch with Seth in the front yard. A little girl who had yet to master sarcasm and wasn't convinced climate change was going to be the end of humanity.

Rebecca's phone started ringing and she stepped away for a moment to answer it. When she ended the call, she said to everyone on the front lawn, "Ngin Ngin is going to be here with Iris in five minutes."

Connor bent his head to whisper in Natalie's ear. "Who's Ngin Ngin?"

"It means 'paternal grandmother' in Toisanese."

"What?" Judy cried. "Ngin Ngin is coming? She's not supposed to be at the rehearsal. No extended family. Iris is only coming because she's the maid of honor."

"Apparently Ngin Ngin stole Iris's phone," Rebecca said, "and refused to give it back unless Iris drove her here from the bed and breakfast."

"Surely Iris could have wrestled her phone back from a ninety-year-old woman without giving in to her demands."

"I don't know," Simon said. "It's pretty easy to injure a ninety-year-old woman, and we wouldn't want that to happen. Especially the night before Rebecca's wedding."

"It's okay." Rebecca came to stand beside her mother. "If it's just Ngin Ngin, there shouldn't be too much drama."

Judy shook her head. "Except Ngin Ngin will tell my mother that she was at the rehearsal dinner, and my mother will be furious she wasn't invited, which could lead to a big fight."

"Don't worry so much, Mom." Rebecca looked around the yard. "Where's Dad?"

Judy sighed. "He's in the basement, putting the finishing touches on your present. Despite my protests, he didn't start it until last week."

"He's *making* my wedding present?"

"You didn't hear it from me."

"Ooh, I wonder what it is!"

Another car pulled up and parked beside the house. An elderly Chinese woman hobbled out, one hand on her cane, the other holding a smartphone up in the air. Seth and Simon hurried over to help her.

"Ngin Ngin," Seth said. "I hear you insisted on coming."

"What else would I do tonight? Sit in the room alone?"

A young woman got out of the driver's seat and rushed around the car. Presumably, this was Iris. "Give me back my phone."

Ngin Ngin handed it over. "Now you won't pay attention to me. Will stare at screen instead."

"You have lots of people to pay attention to you here."

Ngin Ngin looked around, and her gaze landed on Connor. "Who's this?"

"That's Connor," Seth said. "Natalie's date."

Ngin Ngin broke into a grin. She was missing a few teeth. "Natalie, I gave up on you long time ago. But now you have a boyfriend?"

"He's even a doctor," Simon said.

"Doctor and cute? Very nice. Big strong man. Look after you."

"I don't need anyone to look after me," Natalie protested, "and Connor is *not* my boyfriend. I just brought him to the wedding as my date."

"Hmph. Silly girl."

Connor knew that Natalie's father's parents hadn't gone to his wedding, but Ngin Ngin seemed to have no problem with her granddaughters dating white men.

Well, it had been close to forty years, hadn't it? Things changed.

Natalie's paternal grandfather had passed away when they were in university. Connor remembered Natalie going to the funeral in third year, but she hadn't seemed too distraught by the news.

"You could get pregnant before you get married." Ngin Ngin used her hand to show a pregnant belly. "It's okay, Natalie. You're old. Not much time left."

"He's not my boyfriend!"

For some reason, Connor was a touch bothered by the vehemence with which she said that, though he understood her frustration.

Ngin Ngin grinned. "I know. I tease. You must visit me sometime in Toronto. I'm learning to make Italian food! Risotto, tortellini, tiramisu, and…other things I forget. Am friends with an Italian lady. She is teaching me." She turned to Judy. "Where's my son?"

"Howard is in the basement," Judy replied.

"You should get him," Rebecca said, looking at her watch. "It's time to head to the church, and if he's putting the finishing touches on my wedding present, I can't get him myself."

Judy nodded and went back inside. She seemed rather subdued compared to everyone else, even though she was the mother of the bride. Natalie followed her inside with her suitcase, saying she needed to get dressed for the rehearsal.

Fifteen minutes later, they all climbed into their cars and headed across town to the United Church.

"What do you think of my family?" Natalie asked.

Connor turned left onto Main Street. "Two of them said I was cute, so I approve."

She laughed. "Thanks for doing this for me. It's nice to have someone here who isn't related to me."

He didn't feel like he was doing much of anything for her, to be honest.

"No problem," he said.

When he glanced over, there was a faint smile on her lips.

And damn, she was gorgeous in that fuchsia dress.

He found himself raising his hand to touch her shoulder, then quickly returned it to the steering wheel, confused by his reaction.

After the rehearsal dinner, Connor headed to the bed and breakfast, and Natalie returned to her childhood home with her parents and Rebecca. There were five rooms at the bed and breakfast, each named for one of the Great Lakes: Superior, Michigan, Huron, Erie, and Ontario. Connor was in the Ontario room.

The Superior room was, naturally, the nicest room, with a Jacuzzi and a king-sized bed—that was where Elliot was staying. He and Rebecca were sleeping apart the night before their wedding, which struck Connor as old-fashioned. He and Sharon certainly hadn't done that.

And look how their marriage had turned out.

For various reasons, Connor couldn't imagine getting married again, and he didn't have any interest in a serious relationship. He'd dated casually since his divorce, but no woman had captured his interest at all; usually, he felt bored on dates.

However, he wasn't a bitter divorced man who was totally against marriage. He could be genuinely happy at other people's weddings, and Rebecca and Elliot did seem well matched. In fact, seeing them together—as well as Seth and Simon—had caused him a slight pang of longing for something he doubted he'd ever have.

Seth and Simon were in the Michigan room, Iris and Ngin Ngin were in Huron, and Iris's parents, whom he had yet to meet, were staying in Erie. Elliot's family was at the bed and breakfast a few streets over, which was the only other place to stay in Mosquito Bay.

After looking around his room, Connor made himself some tea and headed up to the rooftop patio, figuring he'd be the only one there. It was after ten o'clock.

But Simon was sitting on one of the two chairs, a cup of tea in hand. Apparently, Connor wasn't the only one with this idea.

"Hey." Simon nodded at him. "Come join me. I promise I don't bite."

Connor sat down on the other chair. "Where's Seth?"

"He's asleep. I don't know how, seeing as it's only seven o'clock in Vancouver right now. I'm wide awake."

"Same here." Even though it had been a long day, he wasn't ready to sleep.

"Just reminiscing about my wedding. We were so young, even younger than Rebecca." Simon propped his feet up on the low railing surrounding the rooftop patio. "I smile when I think of that day—that's what I hope for Rebecca, too. Though it took a few years before I could laugh about my mishap with the cake."

"My wedding was nearly perfect." The words were out of Connor's mouth before he realized what he was doing.

Simon's gaze snapped toward him. "Your wedding?"

"I'm divorced."

"Right," Simon said slowly. "So I guess you don't like reminiscing about it?"

"Can't say I do."

"Any children?"

Connor clenched his fingers around the handle of his mug. "No children."

They were quiet for a minute, and then Simon stood up. "I'm going back inside. Don't get drunk on tea." He gave Connor a mock salute before heading down the stairs.

Leaving Connor alone to remember his own wedding, and the day, four years later, when Sharon had taken a pregnancy test because she was finally, *finally* late, after nearly a year of trying.

[4]

Back in her old bedroom, Natalie unpacked her suitcase. Little remained of her early life here. A few books and stuffed animals on the bookcase, but she'd cleaned out the room after she finished undergrad, before moving out to Vancouver to do her PhD. Still, she continued to sleep here whenever she came for a visit.

She sat at her old wooden desk and pulled out her laptop, figuring she'd start reading her student's draft of his master's thesis.

Ten minutes later, she was forced to admit that she couldn't concentrate at all. She kept thinking about the wedding. The rehearsal and dinner had gone reasonably well, and she felt like they were ready for tomorrow. Except in the Chin-Williams family, it was inevitable that something would go wrong, though there was no telling what it would be.

She got up and knocked on Rebecca's door.

"Come in," Rebecca said.

Her little sister was lying on her stomach on top of her bedspread, which was purple with bright yellow and blue flowers. When Rebecca was ten, she'd thought it was the height of coolness. A plastic storage container was open in front of her, and she had a stack of paint chips in her hand.

"I thought you were writing your speech," Natalie said.

"I got stuck." Rebecca nodded at the sheets of lined paper beside her.

Natalie picked them up and looked at what she'd written. "Love conquers all" and various other clichés.

Rebecca had never had a way with words. Her talents lay in math and physics.

For example, if Sarah had 50 strawberries and Billy had 40 watermelons, and they were cycling across the country at 20 km/h, and the slope of the hill was 10°, and the coefficient of friction was 0.5, and everybody's eyes glazed over…

Rebecca could figure out the answer faster than anyone else. She'd studied engineering in university.

She was also fairly artistic. Natalie peeked in the storage container—it was full of art supplies from when Rebecca was a kid, as well as paint chips.

Rebecca handed her a paint chip. "Don't you think the *lemon cream* is pretty?"

"Mm. It is." But Natalie had never been obsessed with colors the way her sister was.

Natalie remembered when Rebecca had discovered paint chips. Rebecca had been eight or nine, and Natalie had been home from university for the summer. Rebecca had burst through the front door after a trip to the hardware store with their parents.

"Did you know they give these away for free at the hardware store?" she'd asked Natalie, holding up the paint chips. "Mom said I could only take three. Will you drive me back tomorrow?"

Rebecca would stare at the paint chips, fascinated by the myriad of colors and the creative names. *Peach jam. Pink magnolia. Autumn maple. Foggy morning.* And since they were, apparently, Canadian paint chips: *Halifax blue, Toronto thunderstorm, Algonquin green*. Natalie had wondered whose job it was to come up with the names. Some didn't describe the color at all. Why was *childhood innocence* a warm, pale pink, and *luxury* a deep purple?

"Look at this one," Rebecca said now, handing another paint chip to Natalie as she sat down on the bed. "The second color matches my wedding dress, don't you think? *Lavender mist*. I love the sound of that."

Since Rebecca had always loved color, she hadn't liked the idea of getting married in white. "Plus I'm hardly pure," she'd said.

Well, Rebecca might not think of herself that way, but she was Natalie's little sister, and that wouldn't change.

There was a knock on the door, and their mother stepped into the room. "I thought we should have a talk about what happens on your wedding night. When a man and a woman—"

"Mom!" Rebecca covered her ears. "Shut up!"

Mom laughed. She'd probably said that just to get a reaction out of her youngest daughter.

"Any other sage advice on marriage?" Rebecca asked.

"Don't go to bed angry," Mom said.

"That's a bit of a cliché," Natalie said, "as is everything else Rebecca has written down for her speech tomorrow. Perhaps she inherited her love of clichés from you."

Mom turned to Rebecca. "You'll figure it out. You always do."

She left the room, and Natalie picked up the sheets of paper again. "What do you want to talk about in your speech?" she asked her sister.

"I want to thank everyone for celebrating with us, thank the wedding party and our parents…mention the great example of love and marriage they set for me…"

"So just say it like that. Don't make it too complicated. Short and simple is best for wedding speeches. You don't want to go on and on."

"You're right." Rebecca smiled at her. "That's what I'll do. I won't try to write any fancy words."

"Are you nervous about tomorrow?" Natalie asked.

Rebecca looked up from a green paint chip. "There's a chance of rain, so I'm a little worried about that, plus you know what weddings are like in our family. But I'm completely sure I want to marry Elliot. Even though we've only been together nine months, I'm sure. I know you think we're rushing it—"

"I just want you to be happy." Natalie had always looked out for Rebecca, particularly when their parents weren't able—or couldn't be bothered—to do so.

"We will be."

"I'll leave you alone to work on your speech now. Let me know if you want me to read it over later, okay?"

"Don't worry, I will."

Natalie hesitated. "I love you."

"Love you, too." Rebecca smiled, then turned back to her paint chips.

~

Twenty-five years ago...

Natalie's little sister was tiny and funny looking and wailing at the top of her lungs, but Natalie loved her anyway. She had always wanted a sister.

"Can I hold her, Mom?"

Her mother had been in the hospital for three days. There were dark circles under her eyes, and she looked like she was about to pass out.

"Okay, honey." Mom's voice sounded flat. "Make sure you support her neck."

Natalie took the baby and held her the way Mom showed her. The baby kept crying.

"Shh," Natalie whispered. "It's okay. It's me! I'm your big sister." She turned to her mother. "Is she hungry?"

"I hope not. I just fed her. Maybe I should change her diaper soon."

Natalie walked around with her baby sister and rocked her back and forth. Eventually, her sister's screams quieted to the occasional sob.

Seth ran up to her and wrinkled his nose. "Why does she cry so much? What's wrong with her?"

"Nothing's wrong with her," Mom said. "It's just the way babies are."

In the next few weeks, however, it became apparent that something wasn't quite right.

As far as Natalie knew, her sister was healthy, although she did seem to make an awful lot of dirty diapers and cry at the most inconvenient times. But something was off with how her parents behaved with the baby.

Natalie didn't know a lot about babies, but she'd seen mothers and their new babies before. The mothers might look tired, they might look frustrated, but they would still snuggle their babies and coo over them and stuff like that.

Her baby sister didn't get any of that from Mom and Dad.

Didn't babies need love and affection? Wasn't that important, in addition to being fed and having their diapers changed?

Natalie had a sinking feeling that she was the only one who loved her baby sister. Had her parents been like this with her and Seth? She couldn't remember, but she didn't think so.

Since nobody else played with the baby, Natalie started showing her stuffed animals and reading her books and taking her for short walks in the stroller. She'd hurry home after school each day to spend time with her little sister. Mom always seemed happy to hand her over, and she showed Natalie how to change diapers. Dad more or less ignored her.

Three weeks after the baby had come home from the hospital,

Natalie finally asked her mother a question that had been bugging her for a while.

"Why doesn't the baby have a name?"

Mom, who was sitting at the kitchen table, sighed as though she had the weight of the world on her shoulders. "I don't know, honey." Her voice still sounded horribly flat and un-Mom-like. "I guess I just haven't given it much thought."

"Doesn't she need a name so you can put it on the birth certificate?"

"The birth certificate." Mom shut her eyes for a moment. "Another thing I have to do." She paused. "Why don't you name her?"

"Okay." Natalie nodded decisively. "I will."

"What are you thinking?"

"You want me to have a name already? I need to do research first."

Mom laughed, but it didn't sound like a normal laugh. "Okay, you do your research. There's a book of baby names on my bookshelf."

Natalie dutifully read every page of the baby name book. Under each name, its meaning was listed along with its origins and sometimes one or two famous people who shared the name. Two nights later, Natalie had a list of twenty-two names she thought were acceptable. Then she carefully went through each name and crossed out any that didn't seem to suit her sister, or that were the same as the names of her classmates or neighbors. She was left with three options.

Although Mom had told Natalie that she could name the baby, Natalie wasn't entirely comfortable with the idea. It wasn't her baby—shouldn't Mom or Dad choose the name? She figured Mom could pick from her short list of three names.

Natalie took the list to her mother, who was watching TV in the living room. Her sister was asleep in the baby swing.

"Here are the names I thought of," Natalie said.

Mom read them out loud. "Lindsay, Alexandra, and Rebecca."

"What do you think? Which one is your favorite?"

Mom shook her head and sighed. "Not Alexandra. How about…Rebecca?"

Natalie knelt on the floor beside the swing. "Hello, Baby Rebecca."

Mom smiled—as much as she smiled these days, anyway. It barely counted as a smile.

"Will Dad be okay with it?" Natalie asked.

"He won't care."

Natalie hesitated before asking her next question. "Mom, are you okay?"

Mom's pregnancy had been rough, and she'd had horrible morning sickness—not restricted to the mornings—for most of it. It had been enough to make Natalie resolve that she'd never get pregnant, though Mom had insisted she'd change her mind when she was older.

Natalie had thought her mother would be better once the baby was born, but Mom still wasn't herself.

Mom sighed once more. "I'm fine. Don't worry about me. I'm just tired because I was up all night with the baby—with Rebecca, I mean."

"Why doesn't she sleep more than an hour or two at once?"

"She'll get better soon. It won't be like this forever."

"I wish I could feed her so you could get more sleep."

"Oh, honey. That's sweet of you." There were tears in Mom's eyes. "But it's okay. You do enough for her." Mom held out her arms, and Natalie let herself be embraced.

Then she went to her room and made a fancy nametag for Baby Rebecca's room with dolphins and starfish and seahorses. Dad had taken Natalie and Seth to Toronto to visit family several weeks ago, and they had seen an IMAX film about the ocean, after which Natalie had decided she wanted to be an oceanographer when she grew up.

For the next few months, it felt like Rebecca was *hers*. Natalie spent hours a day with her. She changed her diapers and gave her baths, and when her mother stopped breastfeeding, sometimes Natalie would feed her, too. And every day, she would read to her.

When Rebecca smiled for the first time, it was for Natalie.

Seth didn't care about his baby sister, but that wasn't a surprise. Boys were silly. But even as Rebecca grew and became more playful, Mom and Dad didn't seem to take the appropriate interest in her.

The summer came, and Natalie spent even more time with her sister. Sometimes she'd play outside with her friends, but a lot of the summer was spent with her little sister, and she delighted in each milestone Rebecca reached.

One day in September, she came home after school and found her dad reading to Rebecca. Not from a picture book, but from one of his hardboiled detective novels. Rebecca giggled when he said "disemboweled."

"She laughs now," Dad said.

"She's laughed for a while."

"Really? I never noticed."

Natalie would usually take care of Rebecca after school, but her father had come home early and was reading to his youngest daughter instead, and that was good. It was the way it should be. Natalie felt a twinge of jealousy, but she was also relieved. She'd gotten a book on the ocean from the school library last week, and she hadn't had a chance to look at it yet. Now she could read it without feeling guilty, without feeling like there was something else she ought to be doing instead. She took out her fancy set of fifty pencil crayons and copied some of the pictures from the book. Such strange creatures lived in the depths of the ocean. She had never been to the ocean, but when you were on the shore, would it look all that different from Lake Huron? You couldn't see the other side of Lake Huron, either. When she was grown up, she was going to travel a lot and see all the natural wonders of the world.

After that day, Dad took more interest in Rebecca. Natalie no longer felt like she was the only one providing Rebecca with love and affection, even if her father's version of love was reading aloud murder scenes. He would also play peek-a-boo and cuddle her in his lap.

Something still wasn't right with Mom, though.

Natalie frequently came home from school to find her mother lying on the sofa or the bed, spaced out but not sleeping. She didn't smile or laugh anymore—it was as though the ability to do those things had been transferred from her to Rebecca.

Natalie asked her father what was wrong with her mother.

"It's difficult being home with a baby all day," Dad said. "That's all."

Perhaps that was true, but Natalie had a feeling this wasn't quite normal.

Rebecca started crawling and walking while holding onto furniture, and Natalie was fascinated by her development. Her parents had a few books on babies, and she read them to make sure Rebecca was developing at the proper rate. She seemed to be doing just fine.

Her first word was "Nattie." Natalie was thrilled when Rebecca started speaking, but she also felt a little uneasy. Shouldn't Rebecca's first word be "Mama"?

Her second word was "murder," thanks to her father.

One Saturday morning that winter, Natalie woke up late and found her mother playing with her sister in the living room. Mom was building small towers out of blocks, and Rebecca was flinging her arms around and knocking them down with glee.

"Who's the sweetest little girl?" Mom said in a high-pitched voice.

Rebecca giggled in response.

Mom spent several hours in bed that afternoon, as though

playing with Rebecca had exhausted her. But over the next few weeks, she slowly showed more affection toward Rebecca, rather than just taking care of her basic needs.

By the following summer, Rebecca had no shortage of attention from her parents and Natalie, and even Seth would play with her on occasion. He was more impressed now that his little sister could "do something other than cry."

Twelve-year-old Natalie was more certain than ever that she was never having kids. Her mother's pregnancy and listless existence for the first year of Rebecca's life scared the crap out of her. She never wanted to go through that herself. Plus, babies were so much work—now she knew *exactly* how much work they were—and although she generally enjoyed looking after her sister, the experience had shown her that it wasn't the future she wanted. She was going to have an exciting career as an oceanographer. No babies for her.

When she was seventeen—and no longer convinced that oceanography was the career she wanted—Natalie read an article in the newspaper about postpartum depression. She realized that was probably what her mother had had after Rebecca was born, though it didn't explain her father's initial apathy toward Rebecca. Was there an equivalent for fathers?

If she had a baby, Natalie wouldn't necessarily get postpartum depression, and if she did, she could get help. But that wasn't enough to make her want children. She liked kids, but the idea of being a mother didn't appeal to her.

"You'll change your mind," Mom said, just like she had when Natalie was younger, and Natalie was frustrated that no one took her seriously.

She went off to university in Toronto when she was eighteen. When her family said their goodbyes in her dorm room, Rebecca, who was seven, threw her arms around Natalie's waist and cried.

"I'll call you every day," Natalie promised.

She didn't need to talk to her parents or brother that often.

But Rebecca was special and always would be.

~

Back in her old room after helping Rebecca with her speech, Natalie picked up an old photo of her and her sister, then put it down and sighed.

It had been years since she'd said "I love you" to anyone but Rebecca.

The last person had been Anthony, a guy she'd dated for six months, and she couldn't help but cringe as she thought of him now. How the hell had she ever believed she loved him? When they'd broken up after the *incident*, he'd said she was too abrasive and pessimistic and a whole bunch of other things.

Anthony was a tool.

And yet.

Her past was littered with failed relationships, and the things he'd said hadn't exactly been out of line with what other men had told her. She'd continued to date for a little while after Anthony, but she'd soon given up.

The whole child-free thing was certainly a problem, when any man who professed an interest in her wanted her to be a mother, and she told herself that was why she didn't bother with dating anymore. That was why she tried not to hope for what Rebecca had. If she didn't hope too much, she couldn't be disappointed.

Sometimes, however, Natalie feared that regardless of that issue, she was simply unlovable the way she was.

She had no interest in giving herself a personality makeover for a man, though. No way in hell was that happening.

But could a guy truly love the real her?

You can be loved, she tried to tell herself. *Think of your sister. You love her, and she loves you.*

Still, she had her doubts.

Her phone vibrated. She grabbed it off her desk and smiled

when she saw the text was from Connor. This would be a good distraction from her depressing thoughts.

How's it going? he asked. *Is Fuzzy Wuzzy happy to see you?*

Natalie glanced at the blue bear that sat on her old dresser, the bear that had been in numerous pretend weddings twenty years ago. *Well, his mouth is sewn shut, so he struggles with facial expressions, the poor thing. But I think he's happy.*

I still can't believe you have a teddy bear named Fuzzy Wuzzy.

I was three years old, she replied. *It seemed like a sensible idea at the time.*

My teddy bear was just called Teddy.

How unoriginal.

I know. Shamefully unoriginal. Maybe I should have called him Beary McBearface.

She chuckled.

You ready for tomorrow? he asked.

As ready as I can be. Something will go wrong, though. I just know it. And don't tell me to be a fucking optimist.

I wouldn't dare.

When Natalie jumped in the shower a few minutes later, she was still smiling, despite everything on her mind.

$$[\ 5\ ]$$

Rebecca practically bounced in her chair as the stylist filled her hair with bobby pins. Natalie thought she was the perfect picture of a blushing bride. Her little sister, all grown up, but with child-like excitement about her big day.

"Don't move," the stylist said.

Rebecca stopped moving and grinned at the mirror.

The hair stylist and make-up artist had come to her parents' house to do Rebecca's hair and make-up, as well as those of the maid of honor and the bridesmaids: Iris, Natalie, and Kelsey, who'd been friends with Rebecca since kindergarten.

The three of them were ready, except for their dresses. They nibbled on tea sandwiches and scones as the stylist worked her magic on Rebecca and Mom made annoying suggestions. The photographer was also in the room, snapping pictures of everyone getting ready. There was something a little surreal about the whole thing.

Natalie wasn't used to being dolled up. She rarely wore make-up, and she usually just pulled her hair back in a ponytail, but today, she had a partial updo, curls spilling over her shoulders.

"Do you remember the first boy you said you would marry?" she asked her sister.

"I bet it was Leonardo DiCaprio," Rebecca said.

"Oh, no. It was Robbie Watson." Natalie turned to Iris. "He was the boy next door, same age as Rebecca. His family moved away years ago."

"How old was I when I said this?" Rebecca asked.

"Four," Natalie said. "You came running inside after playing with him in the sandbox and announced you were going to marry him. Then you asked if I would give you a pony as a wedding present."

"And what did you say?"

"No, of course."

"I bet I was crushed."

"You were," Natalie said. "But I'd long since learned that promising you anything was dangerous because you had a great memory. You were so pissed at me when I didn't get you a dragon for Christmas."

"Robbie Watson," Kelsey said. "You really had a crush on Robbie? The kid was…well, he was kind of weird, to be honest, and way too obsessed with Leonardo. The Ninja Turtle."

"It's news to me," Rebecca said. "I don't remember having a crush on anyone before Johnny Mackenzie in grade one."

"Oh, I don't think you had a crush on Robbie." Natalie shook her head. "You just said you wanted to marry him. I doubt you had any idea what marriage meant."

The stylist started spraying Rebecca's hair with hair spray.

"No! Too much!" Mom said after only two sprays.

"Just do whatever you need to do." Rebecca looked at the stylist in the mirror. "You're the expert. Not my mother."

Mom shot her a glare, but it was an affectionate one. A *you're-exasperating-but-I-love- you-anyway* kind of look. Then she turned her attention to Natalie. "When you were young, you told me you were going to marry Seth when you grew up."

Iris and Rebecca laughed.

Natalie scrunched up her face. "Incest. How lovely."

"And then," Mom continued, "Seth announced he would marry me."

"Isn't that sweet." Natalie picked up an egg salad sandwich and hoped it wouldn't give her food poisoning. Or bad breath.

The stylist slipped a silver hairpin with flowers and tiny leaves into Rebecca's somewhat-messy updo. "All done."

"You look lovely!" Iris said. "Elliot won't be able to keep his hands off you."

"He'd better not ruin all my hard work getting ready," Rebecca said. "Not until tonight." She turned to Iris and Kelsey. "Yesterday, Mom tried to give me a lecture about what happens on your wedding night."

Iris giggled. "I wonder how many people actually have sex for the first time on their wedding night these days. Probably very few."

Hair and make-up complete, they put on their dresses. The bridesmaids' dresses were purple, about two shades darker than Rebecca's *lavender mist* wedding gown. Without a veil and a white dress, her sister didn't quite look like a traditional bride, but with her bouquet of white and pink roses…

She was beautiful.

They took pictures in the backyard, where Rebecca had played with Robbie Watson all those years ago. Where Natalie had entertained her with endless games of buzzball, a bizarre game she'd invented for her sister. Out front, they took pictures beside the large maple tree that Rebecca used to climb as a kid, and in front of the lilac bush that had decided to bloom at just the perfect time this year. There were only a few clouds in the sky, and it didn't look like it would rain—a lovely day for a wedding.

Natalie looked fondly at her childhood home, a non-descript red brick house in a small town on the shores of a lake so wide, it was like the ocean. She didn't return to her hometown all that often, and she'd never want to live here again, but it did have its charms.

They finished up the pictures earlier than expected and headed to the living room.

"Let's look at Mom and Dad's wedding album," Rebecca suggested.

"Really?" Mom said. "You want to look at *that*?"

"Why not?"

Mom didn't say anything.

Rebecca went to pull the small, worn leather album from its place on the shelf.

Except it wasn't there.

"Where is it?" she asked.

"I'll get it for you," Mom said.

Strange. Why would she have moved it? It had been there forever, and Natalie didn't like when things changed in her child-hood home. It should stay the same for always.

Mom came back a couple minutes later, and Rebecca eagerly flipped to the first page of the album, which had three photos of her mother in front of a small church in Toronto. In one of them, she stood beside Aunt Louisa, her maid of honor and the only member of the Williams family in attendance.

But when Natalie looked at the pictures, she didn't see the pain of two people getting married without their parents in attendance, without most of their siblings.

Rebecca flipped to the next page. There was a picture of Mom walking down the aisle by herself—no father to do the honors—and two pictures at the altar.

When Natalie saw these old photographs, with the faded colors and the styles from the seventies, she saw two people who were in love and had gotten married despite everything that was against them.

Still, she was under no illusions that her parents' marriage was perfect.

She glanced at the walls in the living room. They were a pale blue-gray, which, according to the paint chip, was called *Baffin Island mist*. How Canadian.

Natalie remembered the name of the color, even though it had been decades, because her parents had had an argument over what color to paint the room, and it had lasted for days. Mom had wanted *Baffin Island mist*; Dad had wanted some other color that she could no longer remember.

Yet they were still married, and they still loved each other.

On the next page in the photo album were pictures of her parents signing the register, the light coming through the stained-glass windows just perfectly.

Rebecca ran her finger over the bodice of her mother's dress. Long sleeves—you rarely saw that on wedding dresses anymore. When Rebecca was little, Natalie would take out the box with Mom's wedding dress and let her sister look at it.

Natalie's heart squeezed. She wanted Rebecca and Elliot to be happily married for decades, wanted them to smile when they looked at their own wedding pictures.

That was what she wanted for herself, too, but she doubted it would happen.

If only she could find a nice man who didn't want children. Unfortunately, the men who were interested in her were all in a hurry to start a family, or they wanted a stepmother for their children from their first marriage. A man who would not complete her—she didn't need anyone to do that—but who would listen to her rant and rub her shoulders after work and sleep with her at least once a week. Buy her flowers on her birthday. Appreciate and love her for who she was, rather than complain she was too abrasive and pessimistic.

She'd done the sex-without-feelings thing, and that was okay when you needed it, but as much as Natalie was loath to admit it, she also wanted the romance. She rarely went on dates anymore —what was the point?

A few years ago, she'd gone out with a divorced man who had two children. They were three and seven, and she just couldn't imagine living with them. She felt awful about it, felt like she was somehow broken, but she didn't want to be a stepmother.

But she wanted to have what her parents had, what her sister seemed to have with Elliot. To have a wedding day, even if it was a bit of a disaster, that she could look back on in the years to come.

She blew out a breath she hadn't realized she was holding.

It was okay if Rebecca's day wasn't perfect. Natalie wanted it to be—oh, she did—but it was still Rebecca's wedding day, and she was marrying a man she loved very much.

Though Natalie really, *really* didn't want there to be any food poisoning.

Rebecca was now looking at pictures of their parents' wedding reception. One of Aunt Louisa, gesturing animatedly as she gave a speech. Another of Mom and Dad dancing. They looked so young, Dad with his longish black hair…

"Oh my God," Iris said. "Is your father wearing a ruffled shirt?"

"He is," Natalie said, smiling faintly.

She glanced back at her mother, who stood behind the couch. Mom wasn't looking at the wedding photos. No, she was frowning at the *Baffin Island mist* walls.

She's just a little nervous, Natalie told herself. *Her baby is getting married. She's just nervous.*

Connor was sitting in the second pew, next to Seth and Simon. He felt a little strange being so close to the front, given he hardly knew the bride and groom, but Simon had invited Connor to sit with them.

Simon was currently fixing Seth's tie. "You always do it wrong."

"I do not," Seth said. "It's perfectly serviceable."

"It's not supposed to be serviceable. It's supposed to be impeccable. This is your little sister's wedding."

"I wonder if she'll do a face-plant into the wedding cake."

Simon smacked his husband's shoulder, but he was smiling. "Maybe Rebecca will outdo me."

"How would she manage that?"

The music started, and everyone stopped talking and turned toward the doors at the back.

And that was when Connor saw her.

Natalie was the first to walk down the aisle, and she looked positively stunning. Her hair was curled and partially piled atop her head. Her eyes were wide and bright. Her lips were pink. She was wearing a purple dress and carrying a bouquet of white flowers, moving slowly down the aisle to allow the photographer lots of time to take pictures. And that smile…

Jesus. She was beautiful.

And unlike last night, it wasn't a fleeting thought.

Somehow it settled in his chest, became a part of him.

His heart pounded faster as she approached the pews at the front of the church. She kept her gaze straight ahead and didn't look at him. But once she was standing at the front of the church, she caught his eye and winked, and he breathed in sharply.

Get it together, Douglas. It's just Natalie. You've known her for seventeen years.

Kelsey came down the aisle next, followed by Iris. Although they looked nice, they didn't have anywhere near the same effect on him.

Everyone around him rose. The bride must have entered, but Connor hadn't noticed because he'd been looking at Natalie. He stood up and turned back.

Rebecca floated into the room on her father's arm, a big smile on her face. And suddenly he wasn't thinking of Rebecca or Natalie, but of the day ten years ago when he'd stood at the altar and a woman in a wedding dress had walked down the aisle toward him.

It had been a mistake. He hadn't understood what he wanted, and he was angry at himself for not figuring that out sooner.

Rebecca approached Elliot, and Connor didn't feel the need to shout "Don't do it!" or anything like that. Many marriages worked out fine. He hoped theirs would be one of them.

The music ended, and they all sat down as the minister began.

"We are gathered here today…"

Connor's gaze slid back to Natalie and stayed there for most of the ceremony.

Connor waited on the front lawn of the church for Natalie to be done with her duties in the receiving line. Once the last guest had offered their congratulations to the bride and groom, Natalie walked down the stairs toward him, and he put his arm around her and greeted her with a kiss on the cheek.

She stepped back and frowned at him. "What was that for?"

He hadn't really thought about it; it just seemed like the right thing to do. Though what he really wanted was to kiss her lips and ruin her pink lipstick, but he wouldn't.

"I'm your date, aren't I?" he said. "I'm just doing date-ly things."

She looked at him as though he was a total weirdo, her eyebrows slanting down. Somehow, that was a very *Natalie* look. A *WTF-is-wrong-with-you* look.

Strangely, he found it endearing right now.

"I have to stick around for pictures," she said, "but you're welcome to leave. Go back to the bed and breakfast, walk along Main Street—"

"Won't that take about five minutes?"

"Sounds about right. Anyway, you can take off and meet me back at the community center at five o'clock. I don't mind."

He leaned in close, brushing a curl behind her ear. "I'm your date and your emotional support. That's what you want, right? What if a skunk sprays the whole wedding party?"

She put her hands to her face and groaned. "Stop putting wedding disasters in my head."

"What if you sprain your ankle? What if Rebecca gets into a fight with her new mother-in-law? What if you bend down and the back of your dress splits down the middle?"

Actually, the thought of getting Natalie out of her dress was rather appealing.

"Fine, fine," she said, rolling her eyes. "If you really want to watch me blink as the photographer takes my picture, be my guest."

And so he stayed.

[6]

To Natalie, it felt like a miracle.

Nothing had gone wrong when they were getting ready for the wedding this morning, and nothing had gone wrong during the ceremony—the best man hadn't forgotten the rings, and nobody tripped when walking down the aisle.

Nothing had gone wrong during pictures, either. No skunks, no rain, no wardrobe malfunctions. At one point an off-leash dog had run up to Rebecca, and Natalie had braced herself for trouble. But instead, the wedding photographer just got some very cute pictures of Rebecca, Elliot, and a goldendoodle named Tequila Sunrise, who seemed quite happy to pose for pictures. Her owner turned out to be Rebecca's kindergarten teacher.

So far, so good.

Which made Natalie worry that something really bad would happen at the reception to make up for their good luck thus far.

She arrived at the community center at exactly five o'clock, Connor by her side. He'd been unusually attentive to her all day, as though he was taking this date business very seriously. He'd even told her she looked beautiful after she and Rebecca had taken a few pictures together, and that had caused an unexpected flicker of pleasure in her chest.

"This is the first time I've been to a wedding reception in a community center," he said as they walked into the reception room.

"I know it's not very classy."

"Not what I was going to say. It just gives it a very small-town feel." He nodded toward the small bar at one end of the room. "What would you like to drink?"

"Red wine, please."

She looked around the room. There were ten tables, all with white tablecloths, white coverings on the chairs, blue napkins, and pink and white flower arrangements. Near the door, there was a table for gifts, and Iris was getting everyone to sign the guest book.

Natalie had attended many wedding receptions here over the years, including one for Uncle Carey and two for Aunt Louisa.

And now it was Rebecca's turn.

Natalie hadn't had much to do with the planning, since Ottawa was a long way from Mosquito Bay, although Rebecca had texted her pictures and asked for her opinion on several occasions.

"Here you go." Connor returned with her glass of wine. He filled out his gray suit quite nicely, and it looked good with his light blue shirt and dark blue tie.

Just as Natalie was taking her first sip of wine, she heard the click of a camera.

A candid shot. Well, she probably looked *lovely* in that one.

"Okay, you two," said the photographer, a middle-aged woman with short hair and the energy of a bumblebee. "Smile!"

Natalie forced a smile for the zillionth time today.

Except…she didn't have to force it too much. Despite the fear at the back of her mind that something awful would happen, she felt happy, and Connor's arm around her shoulder was nice, too.

Rebecca arrived a few minutes later. She'd gone back to their parents' house to change into a red cheongsam. Many of the Chinese women Natalie knew wore a white dress for the ceremony, then a red dress for the ten-course banquet. Rebecca wasn't having a Chinese banquet, but she did have the dress, which was bright red with gold embroidery and a high neck.

"Beautiful!" Ngin Ngin cried when Rebecca and Elliot approached her. "But flowers…" She clucked her tongue. "Should not have been white." She shook the bride's bouquet and then nodded at the flower arrangement on the nearest table. "Bad luck."

"It's the color of death." Dad shrugged. "Just silly superstitions, of course."

Ngin Ngin gave him a withering glare before walking away.

There was an hour of drinks and appetizers before the buffet dinner in a room full of people who meant something to Rebecca and Elliot. Lots of hugs and congratulations, catching up with people Natalie hadn't seen in ages. There were many family members whom she only saw every few years, at weddings and funerals.

She thought back to the pictures of her parents' wedding. None of her grandparents had come, and even though that was almost forty years ago, it wasn't something that could be forgotten.

Ngin Ngin had apologized profusely for it some time ago, and she'd given Mom and Dad a wedding present a year after her husband's death. It had become clear that Natalie's paternal grandfather—whom they'd called Yeh Yeh, the rare times they saw him—had been the one who disapproved the most of Mom and Dad's marriage, and the one who made all the decisions. Without him, Ngin Ngin seemed happier and more outgoing.

Sad to marry a man you were happier without.

Grandma, on the other hand, had never fully accepted Mom's choice of husband, and they had a tenuous relationship. She and

Grandpa, who'd passed away seven years ago, hadn't gone to Seth and Simon's wedding, either.

Family was complicated.

Natalie snagged a bacon-wrapped scallop off a tray as Grandma and Aunt Louisa approached.

"That was a wonderful wedding." Aunt Louisa swayed slightly, then had a gulp of wine from what was almost certainly not her first, or even second, glass. "And I would know. I got married three times."

Grandma looked at her disapprovingly. She seemed to particularly enjoy being disapproving, and she was very good at it.

"That's an interesting dress," Grandma said to Rebecca. "Is it a kimono?"

"No," Rebecca said. "A kimono is Japanese."

"Hmph." Grandma tapped her cane on the floor before turning to Elliot. "I'm still waiting for my first great-grandchild. I hope you plan on giving me one sometime next year."

He chuckled. "We'll see."

"Natalie is too focused on her career and predicting the end of the world. And Seth—"

"Okay, Grandma," Natalie interrupted, hoping to prevent any inappropriate remarks about her gay brother. "We get it. You'd like a baby in the family."

"I'm not getting any younger. I haven't got all the time in the world."

"And thank God for that," Aunt Louisa said, holding up her glass.

Grandma narrowed her eyes at Aunt Louisa before turning to Natalie. "Who's this you brought with you?"

"His name is Connor," Natalie said.

"Are you telling me you actually have a boyfriend? Why, it's a miracle!"

Her jaw tensed, but she would remain polite. She rarely saw these people, and she didn't want to cause a scene at her sister's wedding. It wasn't the time for the snarky response she was tempted to give.

"Actually, he's just my date." She managed a smile.

"Pleasure to meet you," Connor said, extending his hand.

"You should go out with him," Grandma said. "You're not getting any younger, either. How old are you—thirty-nine?"

"Thirty-six," Natalie muttered.

"Rebecca!" Mom bustled toward them. "Do you need anything? Can I get you another drink? A scallop?"

"I'll take both!" Aunt Louisa said.

Rebecca shook her head. "I'm fine."

Mom winked at her, then hustled Grandma and Aunt Louisa out of the way, toward some of Natalie's cousins.

Natalie flopped down on a chair. She was glad that conversation was over, and she needed to rest her aching feet—she wasn't used to wearing heels. Connor sat down on one side of her, Rebecca on the other. Elliot went off to talk to his aunt and uncle.

"Rebecca, I forgot to ask you," Natalie said. "Are you going to change your name?"

"I think so. I always thought Chin-Williams was kind of awkward, and I want to have the same last name as my kids."

Ngin Ngin hobbled over at the mention of "kids," and Connor offered his chair to her.

"You will have children?" Ngin Ngin said. "Is this what I heard?"

"Rebecca doesn't need to have children just because she's married." Natalie had been so focused on her sister's wedding that she'd forgotten about the possibility of kids. Perhaps Rebecca was already pregnant, and that was why they'd had such a short engagement.

No. Rebecca would have told her.

Wouldn't she have?

"We want kids." Rebecca smiled.

"Good," Ngin Ngin said. "I will babysit for you. You have to bring the baby to my house. Hard for me to travel, but I will look after him whenever you want."

Natalie exchanged a look with Rebecca. Ngin Ngin was ninety and had trouble walking. She probably couldn't pick up a baby…and what if she fell?

"You must have a small baby so I can carry him," Ngin Ngin continued. "I only got to see you twice when you were a baby. Natalie, only once. But now will be different, yes?"

Rebecca nodded. "It will be easy since we both live in Toronto."

However, that wasn't the main reason Ngin Ngin had rarely seen her grandchildren. In fact, when Natalie was a baby, they'd lived in Toronto, too. Had Ngin Ngin still been mad at Dad for marrying a white woman, or was it all because of Yeh Yeh that they rarely saw each other?

That was the thing about weddings. They made you remember all the family drama.

"You can be fun auntie," Ngin Ngin said, patting Natalie's hand. "But Connor is a nice boy. Maybe you should consider?"

Apparently, Ngin Ngin and Grandma agreed on something.

"Connor is just a friend," Natalie said.

Connor put a hand over his heart, as though wounded.

Ngin Ngin laughed as she stumbled to her feet, then turned to Rebecca. "Everyone wants to talk to you because you're the bride. Cannot…" She paused and frowned, as if trying to think of the word. "Cannot keep you to myself." She shuffled off.

Rebecca had a sip of her drink. "She speaks English so much better now. Dad says she's started going to classes at the community center. Well, not English classes, exactly, but there are volunteers to help you practice your English."

When Natalie was younger, talking to Ngin Ngin had been difficult, and she'd often needed Dad as a translator. But now they could actually carry on a conversation. It was impressive how her grandmother had learned English in her old age.

Iris came over and took the seat that Ngin Ngin had just vacated. Although she was only a year older than Rebecca, they hadn't played together much when they were children. Iris's father—Dad's brother, Lewis—hadn't gone to Mom and Dad's wedding, and they hadn't spoken for five years after that. By the time Rebecca was born, they were having occasional holidays together, although the tension at these family events didn't exactly inspire Iris and Rebecca to become close.

But then they'd started engineering at the University of Toronto in the same year, Iris having taken a year off to travel. Without their parents around, Iris and Rebecca had realized that they actually got along quite well.

Now Iris pulled a tiny plastic bag out of her clutch. She raised her eyebrows.

"Iris!" Rebecca shrieked. "Put that away."

"Wouldn't it be hilarious if you got high right before your speech? You'd make good use of the buffet, too."

"You can't be serious."

"Of course not." Iris stuffed the marijuana back into her purse. "Though if you want to do some later…"

"I'll stick to booze on my wedding night, thank you."

Natalie had nothing against weed, although she hadn't indulged in a long time. But now she imagined Iris and Rebecca smoking joints together when they were at university. It wasn't a big deal, but she couldn't wrap her mind around it. This was her baby sister!

"I might need it," Natalie joked. "Find me once the dancing starts. It'll help me get through seeing Mom and Dad on the dance floor."

"Aw," Rebecca said. "It's cute."

Their dancing was cringe-worthy, but if Natalie was honest

with herself, she did think it was cute that they always made it onto the dance floor together.

Aunt Carolyn came over. "Lovely wedding, Rebecca. You look beautiful today."

Uncle Lewis nodded solemnly behind her. He rarely spoke, but his wife was a different story. Since Aunt Carolyn was Chinese, Yeh Yeh had approved of the match, although he'd been unhappy they didn't have any sons.

"Thank you," Rebecca said. "We're so glad you could make it."

"Connor, these are my Uncle Lewis and Aunt Carolyn," Natalie said. "Iris's parents."

They all shook hands.

"So," Aunt Carolyn said, "are you next, Natalie?"

Oh, dear God. She was getting sick of this.

"I doubt it," she said.

"You don't have much time left," Aunt Carolyn continued. "Your biological clock…tick, tick, tick!" She laughed as though that were funny.

Nobody else laughed.

"Mom, stop it," Iris pleaded.

Aunt Carolyn didn't listen. "You don't want to wait until you're forty. It'll be harder then, running around after a little kid."

Natalie gulped some of her wine. Why did people feel the need to say such things to single women in their thirties? She considered saying she didn't want children, but in her experience, it wasn't worth the hassle, and her aunt would probably just think she was a freak. Plus, Aunt Carolyn would ask why not, and Natalie wasn't in the mood to explain her life choices. Nobody asked you to justify why you wanted kids—why did she have to justify her decision?

I don't want to carry a vomit-inducing watermelon in my uterus then push it out of my vagina, thank you. Is that so hard to imagine? And I've dealt with enough diapers and poo explosions, courtesy of my baby sister, to last a life time. I also like having a good night's sleep and traveling the world. I enjoy kids in moderation, but they're exhausting, and I have no interest in living with a small child again. Then they become teenagers... And now you're going to tell me I'm selfish, aren't you? Many of the reasons people have kids are selfish, too, if you think about it.

She wasn't going to say that, not at Rebecca's wedding, not with Aunt Carolyn. She wouldn't see the woman again for a long time—probably not until Iris got married, if Iris was the marrying sort.

Instead, Natalie took a deep breath and imagined she was outside, enjoying nature. Maybe kayaking on the Ottawa River.

"Ngin Ngin said Natalie can get pregnant before she gets married," Rebecca said, which didn't help matters.

At that, Aunt Carolyn took a gulp of her drink. "Career girls." She shook her head. "Maybe Natalie should move to Toronto. Bigger city."

"I just got tenure," Natalie said, "so I'm not going anywhere. I like my life."

"You say that now, but when you're my age and all alone..." Aunt Carolyn gave her a sympathetic smile.

It wasn't like Natalie wanted to be alone, but that was how things had worked out. Did people really need to rub it in?

Deep breaths. It'll all be over soon. Stay calm for Rebecca.

Aunt Carolyn turned to Connor. "I understand you're just a friend."

"I am," Connor said. "Though I can still admit that Natalie looks beautiful tonight, and I'm sure if Natalie wanted a boyfriend, she could have one."

Oh, Connor. Her friend was so sweet, but he didn't know the truth. For starters, she couldn't have a boyfriend unless she changed her mind about kids. Of course, there were men out there who didn't want children, but for whatever reason, those were never the ones who wanted a relationship with her.

And maybe I'm simply not lovable.

Connor took the empty glass from her hand and put it on the nearest table. "Nice meeting you." He nodded at Uncle Lewis, who had been silent the whole time, and Aunt Carolyn. "Natalie and I are going to get some fresh air."

They leaned against the brick wall at the back of the community center. Connor hadn't been able to stand it any longer. The comments about Natalie's age and her ticking biological clock…

Jesus.

And with her family, Natalie didn't stick up for herself and talk back as much as she did with her friends.

He rubbed his hands up and down her bare arms. "How are you?"

"I'm fine," she muttered. "Those silly comments are nothing new."

"That may be true, but they do seem to bother you. At least a little."

She shrugged. "When you're a single woman over thirty-five, some people can't seem to help themselves. They think you're pathetic. It still gets to me, even if I tell myself it shouldn't."

"You're anything but pathetic."

"And that's why you're my friend."

She rested her forehead against his shoulder, and that felt… rather nice, actually. He ran his hand up and down her back, covered in shiny purple fabric. Her fancy hairdo was a bit mussed, but she did indeed look beautiful, as he'd said to her aunt.

He'd meant what he said. If Natalie wanted a boyfriend, he was sure she could have one. She hadn't talked about going on dates for a while, though. There was a time, two or three years ago, when she'd regularly meet people from online dating sites, and then she'd text Connor afterward, sometimes even meet him at the bar after her dates.

Lately? Not so much.

"But otherwise," he said, "it's gone reasonably well. The ceremony was nice, and I bet the pictures will turn out great."

"We haven't eaten dinner yet. There's still time for one of my relatives to stab someone with a fork." She ran her hands through her hair.

"Don't. You'll mess it up even more, and I bet there are more pictures to come."

Though he wanted to mess it up himself. Extract the pins and let it all come tumbling down. The thought seemed so…erotic.

He shook his head.

"It's not the end of the world if something bad happens," she said. "Weddings are rarely perfect. I just want it to be something Rebecca and Elliot can laugh at when they look back on it. Like the Wedding Cake Incident." She blew out a breath. "Let's go back inside."

He placed his hand on her lower back and guided her into the reception, unable to pass up an opportunity to touch her.

Uncle Carey was talking to Rebecca beside the gift table when Natalie walked in with Connor.

"I wish you all the happiness in the world, Rebecca." He hugged her. "I'm so glad we could all be here."

Natalie knew what he was thinking of: the wedding he hadn't attended.

"I just hope you don't put me in the hospital," he said. "Like I did to you at my wedding."

A rather awkward joke, but Rebecca was all smiles. "It wasn't your fault. I hardly remember it now."

Natalie remembered, though. Her little sister had looked so small and fragile in that sterile white room.

"Natalie," Uncle Carey said, startling her back to the present. "I've hardly had a chance to talk to you. How are you doing?"

"Good," she said. "I'm good." *Just a little freaked out that my little sister is actually married, and annoyed with all the comments I'm getting.*

"Anything new with you?"

She smiled. It was easy to smile at him. Uncle Carey was easy-going and good-humored, and she doubted he'd ask if she was ready to pop out babies.

Connor squeezed her shoulder. "Natalie got tenure."

"Did you? That's wonderful."

Yes, she'd managed to get where she wanted in her career, and she was proud of that. She'd even managed to find a position in Ontario. Although Ottawa was a ways from Toronto and Mosquito Bay, she was happy with where she lived.

Uncle Carey went off to join his wife and teenage children, and Connor leaned toward Natalie.

"Did Carey go to your parents' wedding?" he asked. "You said it was just Louisa, but—"

"Uncle Carey seems like a good guy? Yeah, he is. He was only fifteen when my parents got married, too young to drive to Toronto for the wedding. Louisa offered to take him, but his parents said he'd be grounded for the rest of the summer if he went. So he stayed home. I know he feels bad about it."

Just then, Iris walked up to the microphone and asked everyone to take their seats. Natalie would be sitting at the head table, not beside Connor. Unfortunate, because she enjoyed having him here.

Once everyone was seated except for the newlyweds, Iris announced, "Mr. and Mrs. Marsden!" and Elliot and Rebecca walked up to the head table, hand in hand, as people clapped and cheered.

As the buffet dinner was being laid out, the bride and groom cut the cake so it could be served up in time for dessert. They each fed each other a bite, and when Elliot got some icing on his upper lip, Rebecca swiped it off with her finger.

"Use your tongue!" Uncle Dennis shouted, much to everyone's discomfort.

Natalie wondered who'd had more to drink: Uncle Dennis or Aunt Louisa? Hard to say. She glanced at Connor and felt an odd catch in her breath when they shared a smile.

Iris called up one table at a time to get their food, starting with the head table. Once everyone had some sustenance, she gave a short speech, talking about her university days with Rebecca and the phone call she'd gotten after Rebecca's first date with Elliot. The next speech was given by the best man, a close friend of Elliot's. Both speeches were short, funny in places, and heartfelt.

Natalie started to relax. Everything was going pretty well, wasn't it? Not perfect, but pretty good. And hopefully the awkward "are you next?" conversations were finished for her, and she could just enjoy herself.

Yes, maybe her family would get through this wedding without any disasters after all.

She looked at Rebecca, who was lovely in her red dress, and grinned. She was glad that her sister had found love and was having a nice wedding day.

After dinner, Rebecca and Elliot stood up to say a few words before dessert. Natalie had seen her sister's speech that morning —apparently Rebecca had finally put away her paint chips and written her speech last night—and made some minor suggestions. So she knew what was coming.

"Elliot and I would like to thank you all for celebrating our marriage with us. It means so much to have our family and friends here on this special day. Some of you had to travel a long way"—Rebecca glanced at Seth and Simon—"and we're so glad you could make it. Thank you to the bridal party for all your support, and thank you to Elliot's mother, Sherry, for making me feel so welcome and for arranging the wedding favors. Thank you to my parents for helping with the arrangements here in Mosquito Bay." She paused. "Well, let's be honest, ninety percent of that was my mother." A few people chuckled, and she turned to her parents. "Mom and Dad, I also want to thank you for the wonderful example of marriage you've provided me. I always aspired to have a love like yours, and I believe I've found it with Elliot." Dad put his hand over Mom's, but they looked away from each other, probably uncomfortable with the attention. "So once again, thank you all…"

Rebecca trailed off as Aunt Louisa burst into laughter. A loud, high-pitched laugh; she'd always had an annoying laugh, the sort that made you not want to tell jokes in her presence, and it was even worse when she was drunk.

Natalie cringed. *Please don't do anything stupid.*

As everyone looked at Aunt Louisa, Natalie turned her attention to her sister, who was trying to compose herself. But before Rebecca could get any words out, Aunt Louisa said, in a voice just as loud as her awful laugh, "Your parents are getting divorced!"

[7]

NATALIE STARED AT AUNT LOUISA. Why did her aunt feel the need to get wasted at every family gathering? Why did she need to make up such bullshit?

For God's sake, it was Rebecca's wedding!

"I'm serious," Aunt Louisa said, looking around the room. "They want everyone to think they have a great marriage, but they're fucking miserable, and I'm sick of watching my sister live like this. She told me a few weeks ago that they're finally going to divorce, because she started shacking up with this hoity-toity Toronto businessman who has a cottage near Mosquito Bay. And, Mom"—she turned to Grandma—"you'll be happy to hear he's white."

Natalie gripped the table with one hand.

She now suspected her aunt wasn't making anything up.

Aunt Louisa liked to say outrageous things. Then a few seconds later, she would slap the table, laugh that horrible laugh of hers, and say, "Got you there, didn't I?" Even though everyone had known the whole time that she was making shit up.

This time was different.

Plus, she was Mom's confidante. They'd always been close.

Natalie felt silly for thinking, not long ago, that her family might actually get through the wedding without any disasters. She should have known that would never happen.

Aunt Louisa continued. "They would have split up sooner, but—"

"Stop it, Louisa," Mom hissed from the next table over, but she didn't say it was a lie.

Aunt Louisa kept talking. "They didn't want to do it right before your wedding, Rebecca." She burped. "Congratulations, by the way. I'm all for marriage. And divorce. I've done both three times." She held up her empty glass. "Cheers!"

The room was quiet. Everyone was probably too shocked to speak.

How could this be happening? How could Mom and Dad be *miserable* together?

Natalie had never thought her parents' relationship was a fairytale love story, but she'd believed in their marriage. She felt like her understanding of love was crumbling.

At her own sister's wedding. Only hours after Rebecca had tied the knot.

Poor Rebecca.

Natalie's gaze shifted to her sister, who slowly lowered herself to her seat, one hand to her mouth, the other gripping Elliot's arm.

Natalie wanted to gather Rebecca in her arms, like she'd done when her sister was little, and tell her everything would be okay. There were no trolls in the closet, that was just her imagination, she was safe and sound.

At the same time, Natalie wanted to be next to Connor and feel his comforting hand on hers. Something solid to hold on to when it felt like there was nothing solid in this world. She glanced at him, and he gave her a closed-lip smile.

"I told you." Grandma tapped Mom on the shoulder with her cane. "I told you it was a stupid idea to marry that silly boy, just because he reminded you of Bruce Lee. And I was right! It didn't work out."

Ngin Ngin shot to her feet and marched over to Grandma as best she could. "My son is a great man. Why are you listening to these lies? No divorce."

"I didn't tell any lies," Aunt Louisa said.

"You fool." Ngin Ngin turned to Dad. "Tell everyone. It's not true."

Dad whispered something in her ear, and her eyes widened.

"This is your fault." She raised her cane above her head and lunged toward Grandma, who hobbled out of her chair.

Before Ngin Ngin could do any damage, Seth pulled her back, and Uncle Carey pushed Grandma back into her seat.

Damn. It was a near thing that there hadn't been a physical fight between two nonagenarians. Only in the Chin-Williams family could this sort of thing happen.

"My mother might be a racist turd of a human being," Aunt Louisa said, "but this divorce isn't her fault. Just didn't work out, okay? None of my marriages did, either."

"Okay, okay," Iris said, speaking into the microphone. "That's enough. Welcome to our loving family, Elliot! We're really not so bad, but if you need any drugs to get you through the evening, find me and I'll hook you up."

A number of wedding guests chuckled, desperate for laughter. Aunt Carolyn, however, looked more horrified by her daughter's mention of drugs than she had by anything else.

"Anyway," Iris continued. "Howard and Judy, would you still like to say something?"

Oh, dear God. Mom and Dad were supposed to speak.

This would certainly be delightful.

Mom made her way up to the front and took the microphone from Iris. She looked pointedly at Dad, but he remained in his seat, arms crossed over his chest.

"We're so proud of you, Rebecca," she said, a slight tremor in her voice. "You always did well in school, and then you went on to become an engineer..."

Mom continued talking, telling stories about Rebecca as a kid, about meeting Elliot for the first time at Thanksgiving.

"And this is when I was going to say..." She laughed awkwardly. "This is when I was going to say that I know what makes a strong marriage because I've been in one for thirty-nine years, and I want Rebecca to know the happiness that I have. But now you know that's all a crock of shit. So, Rebecca, don't be like us, okay? Be like...Carey and Melanie? Seth and Simon?" She laughed again. "But what do I know? They could be faking it, too. So, other than the don't-go-to-bed-angry advice I gave you last night, I also want to tell you that if it doesn't work out, it's okay. Don't hold on to something just because you're stubborn and you want to prove people wrong. I wish you and Elliot every happiness, but if it's not meant to be, don't spend decades trying to keep up appearances, just to have it all come out at your daughter's wedding. We were going to separate last year, but then Howard convinced me to wait until our mothers died, and really, how much longer could that be?"

"Aiyah!" Ngin Ngin said. "I'm healthy as an ox. Will live many more years. Ten great-grandchildren. Rebecca, you start working on that tonight."

Natalie wanted to sink into the floor. She looked out at the friends and family Rebecca had thanked, not long ago, for coming, and she wished they would all vanish.

Except Connor. He could stay. She didn't want to be *all* alone, but she wanted someone who wasn't related to her.

Mom wasn't done yet. "And then I decided I couldn't wait any longer. I was planning to move out this spring, but you announced you were engaged, and I didn't want to do that to you right before your wedding. I guess we succeeded, since you didn't find out until afterward!"

Oh, God. What a horror show.

"Judy," Elliot said quietly, "how about I walk you back to your seat, and my mother can say a few words."

When Sherry came up to the front of the room, she looked at everyone in stunned silence for a moment before pulling out a folded piece of paper from her purse. She spoke fondly of Elliot, and how much she wished his father—who had died of a heart attack a few years ago— could be here, and then she thanked Rebecca's family for planning the wedding. She made no reference to what had just transpired, instead sticking to her script.

It was good Rebecca had a normal mother in-law. She would probably need it.

"Okay!" Iris said, artificially upbeat. "I think we've given them lots of time to cut the cake. We'll have tea and coffee and wedding cake, and then we'll start the dancing!"

Rebecca and Elliot had their first dance as a married couple. Next, Rebecca danced with Dad while Elliot danced with his mother. Natalie tried to focus on them and forget everything else, but it was impossible.

When the song finished, Iris invited all the guests onto the dance floor. Natalie didn't plan to dance, but she immediately jumped up and made her way toward Connor, thankful she'd had the forethought to bring a date who was here just for her and wasn't wrapped up in the rest of the drama.

However, before she could reach Connor, she was interrupted by her father.

"May I have a dance with my other daughter?" he asked.

"Uh, sure," she said.

Dad took her hand. "Will I ever get to do this at your wedding? I hope you haven't given up on finding love."

She couldn't help but laugh at the absurdity of his words. "You just had your divorce announced at Rebecca's wedding, and you're telling me not to give up on love?"

He shrugged.

Natalie didn't say anything for a while. The lights in the room had been dimmed, and camera flashes went off here and there.

"I only heard Mom's point of view," she said at last. "What about yours? Were you unhappy, too, or not until she started cheating on you?"

"We'd both been unhappy for a while." He sighed. "It's complicated. Don't hold the fact that she found someone else against her. We had agreed it would be okay if…" He shook his head.

Oh, God. Did Mom and Dad have an open marriage?

"Let's not talk about this," he said. "It's supposed to be a happy day."

"Too late," she muttered, but she didn't ask any more questions.

As soon as the song ended, she found Connor.

"What do you need?" he murmured, squeezing her hand. "Another drink? A dance? A trip to Bali?"

"If only. A little fresh air will have to do."

She dragged him outside and around to the back of the community center, where she leaned against the brick wall and sighed.

"My parents are getting divorced," she said. "My parents are getting divorced." It still didn't seem real, like it was a bad dream and she would wake up any minute.

But she knew it wasn't a dream.

Connor braced his arms against the wall on either side of her, like he was protecting her from the world. "I'm sorry."

"It shouldn't bother me so much. I'm grown up; I'm not a child whose life will be upended."

"Of course you're upset. It's okay to let yourself feel that."

"You should be a therapist."

"I'm not going back to school to get another degree."

"I bet you have a great bedside manner. Are you thinking of me as a patient right now?"

"No, I'm here as your friend." He brushed his thumb over her cheek. "Whatever you need."

Whatever you need. For some reason, that sent a shiver through her.

"My father asked if he would ever get to dance with me at my wedding," she said. "I can't imagine what would happen if I got married. Maybe an alien invasion? A zombie attack?"

"Natalie!" It was Rebecca.

Connor stepped back from Natalie, and she immediately missed his body heat.

Rebecca was followed by Iris, Seth, and Simon. They all looked at each other, and then Iris started laughing manically. Everyone else soon joined in.

Once Natalie started laughing, she couldn't seem to stop. She felt rather unhinged.

"Nobody will ever forget your wedding, Rebecca," Iris said between laughs.

"No, they won't."

Iris pulled out her bag of weed. "This sounds pretty good now, doesn't it?"

"Put that away," Rebecca said. "I don't want to smell like pot, and I don't want to be high on my wedding night."

"Come find me after the reception, Iris," Simon said. "I'll smoke up with you, and I might be able to convince Seth to join us."

"Did you see my mother's face when I mentioned drugs?" Iris started laughing again. In fact, she was laughing so hard, she was practically crying. Then she enveloped Rebecca in a hug, and they tottered on their heels. When Iris stumbled, Natalie grabbed her shoulders. The three of them slid to the concrete in a laughing mess while Connor, Seth, and Simon looked on.

Rebecca stood up, but Iris and Natalie stayed on the ground, their legs stretched out in front of them.

"It's a bridesmaid dress," Iris said. "I probably won't wear it again, so who cares."

Rebecca fingered the sleeve of her red cheongsam. "I'm not sure I'll wear this again, but I want it to look nice in the closet."

"When you look at it," Natalie said, "you'll remember Ngin Ngin threatening to hit Grandma with a cane."

"True. Maybe I should just burn everything." Rebecca looked down at her hand and twisted her wedding band. "Did you have any idea they were getting divorced?"

Natalie shook her head. "I never thought they had the world's perfect marriage, but I thought… They were Mom and Dad. They would always be together."

Connor leaned over and put a hand on her shoulder, and she spread her fingers over his.

"When I was here at Christmas," Seth said, "I noticed Mom had some clothes in the dresser in my old bedroom, and I wondered if she'd been sleeping in there."

Natalie felt so naïve. When it came to her parents, she'd always focused on the fact that they were an interracial couple who'd encountered so much disapproval and yet had gotten married despite it and stayed married. She'd tried not to think much of things like the *Baffin Island mist* fight, telling herself that all couples fought.

Which was true. But did most couples have week-long fights about paint colors?

And then there was what had happened after Rebecca was born. Mom had struggled, and Dad hadn't been there for her.

When, exactly, had they realized they'd made a mistake? Did one of them realize it long before the other?

Natalie looked at Connor, as though he might have the answers, though of course he didn't.

"Isn't marriage a wonderful institution?" Iris asked. "Aren't you happy to be a part of it, Rebecca?"

"Better get started on those ten children," Natalie said.

They all laughed some more, because it was better than anything else.

Before they returned to the reception, Natalie pulled Rebecca aside and asked if she was okay, if there was anything she needed from her big sister, and Rebecca shook her head with a bittersweet smile.

At eleven o'clock, Rebecca decided she wanted to return to the bed and breakfast and…

Frankly, Natalie didn't want to think about what her sister would do with Elliot.

Before Rebecca headed out, she had to toss the bouquet. All the single women gathered on the dance floor, even Aunt Louisa, who had three divorces under her belt.

Natalie didn't want to catch the bouquet—it was nothing more than a silly tradition—but she knew someone would drag her up if she didn't go willingly. She stood near the back, figuring Rebecca wouldn't throw it all that far, and didn't bother raising her hands.

Rebecca threw the bouquet—with the white flowers that Ngin Ngin had said were bad luck—and to Natalie's surprise, the flowers hurtled to the back of the room, toward Kelsey, who reached for them.

But then all of a sudden, the flowers were heading toward Natalie, as though they'd magically changed directions in the air. She had to put her hands in front of her face so she wouldn't get hit in the head, and somehow, she caught the bouquet.

How wonderful.

All night, she'd felt like she had a gigantic neon sign that said,

"She's running out of time!" sticking out of her fancy updo, and now the bouquet couldn't help but obey.

She looked at the flowers and wrinkled her nose. Yeah, after tonight, getting married was just what she needed. Not that she believed in any of these stupid superstitions anyway.

Natalie stood near her sister as Rebecca and Elliot said goodbye to everyone. Most people pretended the Divorce Incident hadn't happened. They said it was a lovely wedding, Rebecca looked beautiful; surely, they would have a happy life together.

But not everyone.

"Sorry about that," Aunt Louisa said, swaying as her son and daughter tried to support her. "Though you were gonna find out eventually, weren't you?" She slapped Rebecca's shoulder.

"Congratulations," Grandma said, "on making a better choice than your mother."

"Fuck ya!" Uncle Dennis said, and Natalie had no idea what he was talking about. He probably didn't know, either.

"Remember," Ngin Ngin said, her hand on Rebecca's shoulder. "Ten great-grandchildren. Maybe you start with triplets?"

Connor came up to Natalie after the newlyweds had left, and despite everything that had happened, she smiled when she saw him.

"Do you want to head out?" he asked.

She nodded, then remembered where her stuff was. "Oh, God. I'm supposed to stay at my parents' house."

No way in hell was she doing that tonight. Her parents would have a big fight that would last for hours, and then they would go to bed angry in separate bedrooms.

"Can I stay with you?" she asked Connor.

[8]

Connor's heart started thumping quickly after Natalie's question. He couldn't help but imagine standing behind her as he unzipped her dress, slipping the straps down her arms…

And later, sliding inside her.

But he was pretty sure that wasn't what she had in mind.

"I'm not suggesting anything would happen," she said quickly, "but I can't stay at my parents' house tonight. I just can't. I have friends in town, but it's too late to call them and ask to stay the night. I suppose I could ask Uncle Carey, but—"

"Natalie," he said, grasping her shoulders, "you can stay with me, as long as you're okay with sharing a queen-sized bed."

"That's fine." She looked down at the two bouquets in her hands. Her own bouquet and the larger one that had been Rebecca's. "Let's walk to the park before we go back to the bed and breakfast."

He took the smaller bouquet from her and clasped her hand in his as they walked out of the community center, unable to help himself from touching her.

Natalie led him west. They sat down on a bench in a small

green space, looking out at Lake Huron, and didn't say anything, though he continued to hold her hand.

As soon as Louisa had interrupted Rebecca's speech, Connor had known it was true. Judy and Howard were separating. He'd immediately turned his gaze to Natalie and could see the disbelieving shock behind her calm expression, could see the exact moment she realized it wasn't a lie. Ever since, all of his thoughts had been on Natalie. On being there for her.

"I figured something would go wrong at the wedding, but I never guessed it would be something like this." She shook her head. "I thought maybe Grandma and Ngin Ngin would have a fight, actually—that, I had predicted. Sort of. You know this was only the third time they'd met, even though Mom and Dad have been married for decades?" She let out a bitter laugh. "And to think I made a note to plan their fortieth anniversary!" She took out her phone and held up the note she'd written for herself. "So, yeah, my grandmothers having a fight wasn't much of a surprise, but what they were fighting about *was* a surprise. If only Rebecca had fallen on top of the wedding cake instead and gotten buttercream on her cheongsam…"

Connor put both of the bouquets on the far side of the bench and turned Natalie so she was looking away from him. He started massaging her shoulders.

"I can't believe I caught the bouquet," she said. "I swear it was heading toward Kelsey and then changed directions."

"It was heading toward you the whole time. Maybe you had a bit too much wine."

"I didn't drink enough wine. I'm practically sober."

"Perhaps you'll meet a charming prince when you get back to Ottawa," he said, then experienced a slight pang as he imagined her with a cartoon prince on a cartoon white steed, even though the thought was ridiculous.

Natalie snorted. "Unlikely."

"Maybe you'll meet a charming Member of Parliament."

"Knowing my luck, I'll meet a charming but morally corrupt politician who thinks I'm 'exotic looking' and doesn't believe in global warming."

"That's the dream, isn't it?"

He rubbed her shoulders in silence for a minute. Natalie tilted her head to the side and moaned. That moan put dangerous thoughts in his head.

"I bet you thought I was a paranoid freak when I asked you to come to Rebecca's wedding because I was certain something bad would happen."

"I've never thought of you as a paranoid freak."

"Really? Even when I said we'd be living in a dystopian hell within fifty years and humanity is doomed?"

"Lots of people feel that way right now." He moved his hands down her back. "You're not a complete pessimist, though. You believed in your parents' relationship, didn't you?"

"Yeah, I stupidly did. I believed in love, and it was partly because of them. I was a sap."

Behind her, he smiled. "You're a caring person."

She snorted again. "I don't think most people see me that way."

He wasn't sure, but it was clear to him, especially when he saw her with her sister. Natalie had a cranky, sarcastic side, but she was also a bit of a romantic, and she was devoted to the people she loved.

Right now, he found it an irresistible combination.

Especially with her dark hair—nearly as dark as the night—curling over her shoulders. He pushed it aside so it wouldn't get in the way of his massage, and he ached to tangle his fingers in it.

"Do you believe love can last?" she asked. "Or do you think it's destined to fade in long-term relationships, but people stay together because, well, inertia?"

"I'm sure it lasts. Not for everyone, but it does."

"Even though your own marriage ended."

He didn't say anything, just pushed his thumb into a particularly tense spot on her shoulder.

"Why did it end?" she asked. "You never told me."

No, he hadn't. He hadn't told many people, and he didn't plan to change that now. "I don't want to talk about it."

"That's okay. You don't owe me an explanation."

There was a small part of him that wanted to tell her, but he didn't know what she would think of him afterward. So, he changed the topic.

"You haven't told me about your dating life lately," he said. "A few years ago, you were really serious about the whole online dating thing. You'd go on a date every week or two, and then you'd text me afterward and maybe we'd meet for a beer, and you'd laugh about how bad it was."

"Oh, yeah. I remember that. The guy who said he loved me after only two dates...the guy who sent me a dozen dick pics after two dates. The guy who shouted at me for refusing to sleep with him on the first date, because he thought a woman owed a man after forcing him to sit through a delicious meal and scintillating conversation."

"I can't imagine the conversation was scintillating with him."

"It wasn't. But I'm capable of scintillating conversation."

"I know you are."

"I would meet you afterward, and I would tell you about my bad dates, as well as the men who contacted me online who were so awful that I refused to meet them. It was depressing, but I laughed to make myself feel better, and I tried to see it as absurd. Kind of like tonight." She turned toward him.

He dropped his hands from her shoulders. "You deserve better."

The corner of her mouth quirked up.

"Why don't you tell me about your dates anymore?" he asked.

But then he realized it would pain him to hear about them, in a way it hadn't before. And surely she was dating. In his experience, women in their mid-thirties were usually dating rather desperately.

To his surprise, she said, "I haven't been on a date in months. I stopped believing love could happen for me."

It also pained him to hear those matter-of-fact words.

Though in all honesty, he kind of felt that way about himself. He just hated that she would think that way, too, even if he was a bit relieved she hadn't been seeing anyone lately.

"When did that happen?" he asked.

"About two years ago." She shrugged, trying to pretend it was no big deal. "Just the way it is. The guys who were interested in me were either complete tools, or they wanted different things than I did. After almost twenty years of trying and failing, I realized I had to accept it. And it's okay. It really is." Her voice trembled, just slightly. "I mean, now that my parents are splitting up, I'm reluctant to believe in love for anyone, not just myself.'"

"It's only been a few hours," he said. "It'll take a while to wrap your head around it."

"Will my parents sell the house? Will they both stay in Mosquito Bay? Will we need to have separate holidays? Everything has been the same for so long, and now it won't be."

"They're still your parents."

"Yes. And I can't help wishing I knew exactly what happened, even if a part of me doesn't really want to know. But I want to understand everything. I like having answers."

"I know."

She tipped her head to the side and rested it against his shoulder. They looked out at the dark lake and the stars in the sky.

"Have you dated since your divorce?" she asked.

"I've been on a few dates in the past year, but that's all. I don't have much interest in it."

"But you're a catch! You're a doctor. And you're tall. Women like tall men. You've also got a full head of hair." She paused. "You're rather handsome, in fact."

He lifted his eyebrows and placed his hand on her cheek, tilting her gaze toward him. "You think I'm *rather* handsome, not *very* handsome?"

"Don't want my compliments to get to your head," she said lightly, but her cheeks turned pink.

"So you do think I'm very handsome."

Somehow, nothing else had ever made him feel so delighted.

"Yes," she whispered. "I do."

He dipped his head toward hers, and when she gave him a slight nod, he brushed his lips against hers.

So soft.

When he ran his tongue along the seam of her lips, she opened for him. Her mouth pressed against his, and his tongue stroked hers, and he slipped his fingers into her mass of curls, as he'd longed to do all day. The real thing—it didn't disappoint. He wanted this, and he wanted more.

"Well," she said, pulling back slightly.

"Well," he said.

"I didn't expect that."

Their mouths were close together, but he didn't want any space at all between them.

He cupped her ass and picked her up, settling her on his lap. Now he could wind his arms around her as he kissed her again, as his mouth joined with hers and he tried to make her forget about all that had happened.

"Connor!" She laughed like she didn't know what else to do.

"If you don't like it," he said, "then tell me to stop, and I promise you, I'll stop." He pressed a kiss to her jawline. "But I don't think that's what you want."

Natalie was in his arms, kissing her way down his throat, and it was all a bit surreal. When she reached the top of his shirt, she loosened his tie and unbuttoned the top button, kissing the spot at the base of his throat that had been covered all day. He inhaled gulps of air before dipping his mouth to hers and claiming it again.

She was all that mattered.

~

Natalie couldn't wrap her mind around this. She'd known Connor Douglas for seventeen years, and she'd never considered kissing him before. But now her lips were on his.

How? Why?

She pushed those questions aside. They didn't matter, because this was exactly what she needed after Rebecca's wedding reception.

His mouth was gentle, yet firm. Playing her perfectly. As the kiss deepened, she adjusted herself so she was straddling his lap, pressing her chest against his to get *more*. More of the glorious sensations he caused to spread throughout her body. More of everything.

But when his erection pressed between her legs, she jolted back in shock.

"You want…" She jumped off the bench, vibrating with energy.

His lips quirked up. "Yes, Natalie? What is it that I want?"

She took in a deep breath as her inner muscles clenched. Five minutes ago, they'd been talking, she'd asked if he'd dated since his divorce, and then she'd told him he was rather handsome. That was how they'd gotten here.

Sort of. She wasn't exactly sure how it had happened.

Connor stood up. He curled one hand around hers and placed his other hand on her waist. He stepped to the side and then back, swaying his hips.

"We didn't dance at the reception," he said, "though it wasn't because I didn't ask."

"Did my rejection hurt your feelings?"

He pouted, and it was cute to see this giant of a man pout.

"You're making up for it now," he said.

"I don't like dancing."

"Never?" He slipped his hand inside the top of her dress and flicked her nipple with his finger.

Awareness radiated out from the taut peak of her nipple, and then he covered her breast with his hand.

"Do you like it now?" he asked, still swaying his hips.

"Touching your partner's breast isn't dancing. It's not something you can do in public."

"Ah. So you like *private* dancing."

Her head was spinning. She didn't know what was going on now.

But she wanted him.

"You're trying to seduce me," she said.

"Is it working?" His voice was soft. She felt it on her cheeks and the bare skin above the neckline of her dress.

"Yes," she admitted. "You know it is."

She shifted both of her hands behind his neck, and his hands circled her waist. The night air was cool against her warm cheeks. His lips covered hers again, and she kissed him back, their lips melding together, and *yes*, it felt so damn good.

"The moment I saw you walking down the aisle," he said, "I wanted you. You've been driving me crazy all day."

"All day," she repeated faintly.

It had been a long time since a man had touched her like this —or even kissed her quickly on the lips. A *very* long time since she'd driven a man crazy.

"Just today?" she asked.

He hesitated. "Yes."

This was just for tonight, and that was okay.

Two friends finding solace in one another. Skin against skin, arching bodies, heavy breathing. Just for a little while.

Parts of her life were crumbling, but she could hold on to him. He'd always been there for her, though never like this.

His hands slid to her ass. He lifted her up so her lips were at the same height as his, and he kissed her some more. She wrapped her legs around him and felt his hardness at the juncture of her legs.

"Connor," she moaned.

He continued to work magic with his lips and tongue. She didn't feel like herself, making out with a man in a public park, being pleasured as though she were a beautiful young woman, rather than someone who was supposed to be desperate to settle down because her biological clock was ticking.

Instead, she simply felt desirable.

"Are you sufficiently seduced to come back to my room?" he asked quietly, sliding his lips down the curve of her neck.

She arched against him. "Yes. God, yes."

[9]

Back at the bed and breakfast, Connor sat Natalie down on the bed and kneeled behind her, taking out all the pins in her elaborate hairdo.

She didn't need him to do this; she'd rather he pull her dress over her head immediately. Hell, he could tear it in half if he wanted. It wasn't like she was going to wear it again.

But he insisted. Slowly, he placed one pin at a time on the night table beside the bed, and curls tumbled to her shoulders. She couldn't see him behind her; she could only feel his presence.

"That was the fourth time I've had my hair done," she said, needing to fill the silence. "The first time was for prom, and I was a bridesmaid two other times."

"I've never had my hair done."

She giggled like a schoolgirl. "If my hair is rather stiff, it's from all the hairspray to hold it in place."

When he dropped another bobby pin on the night table, she looked at his large hands, the ones that had been exploring her body and would soon touch her bare skin. *Everywhere.*

She shivered.

"Are you cold?" he asked.

"No," she whispered. "It's not that."

"Have you changed your mind?"

She shook her head.

"Let me take care of you tonight," he said. "Let me give you whatever you need."

She nodded, somewhat dazed, and her breath hitched. Nobody took care of her; they assumed she didn't need to be taken care of.

"I think I got them all." He set the final bobby pin on the table, and then he moved his hand to the zipper at the back of her dress and slowly pulled it down, kissing the skin he'd just exposed as he went.

He turned her around to face him, slipped the straps of her dress down her arms, and unhooked her bra.

"There," he said. "Perfect."

He took one of her nipples in his mouth. His hand moved to her other breast, caressing the pebbled skin before he pinched the nipple between his fingers. She released a shocked little cry.

"How long has it been since a man made love to you?" he asked.

She didn't know how to answer. It had been two years since she'd last had sex, but he'd said *made love*.

The room was dim. Only the lamp on the night table was on, casting shadows over his face.

"Natalie?" he said.

"Too long. It's been far too long."

He laid her down, her head on the pillow. Then he kissed her, his weight pressing down on top of her, and she couldn't help but squirm. God, she loved being underneath him.

And then she remembered…

"Condom," she said.

She didn't have one, and she doubted he'd expected this to happen, either.

"I have a condom." He brushed his lips over her cheek. "Don't worry."

He lifted her skirt and slipped his hand between her legs, against the wet fabric of her panties. He inhaled swiftly and slid the crotch aside, running his finger up and down her slit. She clenched the sheet in her hands as he pushed two fingers inside her and curled them upward. The pleasure of someone else touching her after years of doing it all herself was almost overwhelming.

His hands left her to tug her underwear down her legs. He slipped them off, along with her high-heeled shoes, and shifted so he was lying on his stomach between her legs. She breathed heavily in anticipation.

His tongue touched her clit. Just a light touch, then firmer as his mouth slid down, around her entrance. She bucked her hips against his mouth, and he continued to pleasure her with his tongue. He added his fingers, sliding inside her again.

So intimate, this act. An intimacy she hadn't allowed anyone in a long time, and yet she was allowing Connor.

He circled his tongue over her nub, and as he stroked inside her, she spiraled up and up…and then clamped a hand over her mouth to stifle her cry as she came for him.

He slid up the bed, a crooked grin on his face, and lifted her up so he could remove her dress, which was bunched around her waist.

"Better," he said, once she was naked on her back before him.

But he was fully clothed, and that was a real problem for her. She slipped her hands under his jacket, and he got the hint and shrugged it onto the floor. Next, she pulled off his tie before she started working on the buttons of his shirt, revealing one inch of his chest at a time. Revealing more and more of his strength—she could feel the power of him. When the shirt joined his jacket on the floor, she ran her hands over his upper arms. Earlier, he'd picked her up so easily.

"Not bad," she said as she admired him.

He raised an eyebrow. "You're practically drooling. Looks like it's more than *not bad*."

"My God, you're vain."

He laughed before taking one of her hands in his and moving it to his crotch. She touched his erection through his pants, and he hissed out a breath.

There was no laughter between them now.

Natalie undid his belt and pulled down the zipper on his pants, her hand shaking slightly. Then she pushed her hand inside his boxers and wrapped her fingers around the hot length of him.

"Where's that condom?" she asked.

He was out of bed in a flash and returned a moment later with a square packet. He placed it on the bedside table before he dropped his pants to the floor, followed by his boxers.

She licked her lips at the sight of him, jutting toward her. His gaze never left hers as he got onto the bed, one knee on either side of her hips. She reached for the condom and rolled it on, and then he opened her with his fingers once more, preparing her to take him. The lamp cast half of his face in light, the other half in shadow, as though he were wearing half a mask. It was Connor, her friend of many years, and yet it wasn't—she'd never wanted Connor like this before.

He notched his erection between her legs, and she gasped.

"Good gasp?" he asked. "Or bad?"

"Good. Very good."

She loved the pressure of him, so close to being where she needed him. She was desperate for more, but at the same time, she liked that he was taking it slowly, the pleasure gradually unraveling within her.

He pushed inside, inch by inch, taking her where no man had been in a long time.

"Yes," he whispered. "Natalie." He looked down from above her.

Her lips parted. When she nodded, he started to move. Rolling his hips in a steady pace, stroking in and out of her in the most intimate of ways.

She pulled him down so she could feel his skin against her skin, and he crashed his lips down on hers, exploring her mouth, exploring her response to his every action. She crossed her ankles at his lower back, trying to bring him even closer.

"You're so fucking sweet," he said.

Dimly, at the back of her mind, she found that amusing; nobody ever described her as sweet. But then he pushed deeper, shoving that thought away. Whatever he said and did, she would take it; she would accept it as it was.

He adjusted the angle so he rubbed against her clit on each stroke. His mouth was back on hers now. She started climbing to the precipice, her breathing harsh, her body strung tight with the need to go over the edge.

"Connor," she gasped, wrenching her lips from his.

"Yes, sweetheart. I've got you."

He licked the tip of his finger, and then his hand was between them, running over the place where they were joined.

She needed to see it. Needed to see him entering her over and over. She pushed at his shoulder. He raised himself above her, and she watched his cock move in and out, watched herself take it all and wring so much pleasure from it.

He touched his wet finger to her clit. She jerked in response and rubbed herself against him, whatever she could do to get what she needed.

And yet the intensity of her orgasm caught her off guard. He lowered himself to her as she cried out, and she bit his shoulder in her enthusiasm. He pushed inside her again and again, and soon he was groaning with his own orgasm. She shuddered as he finished inside her.

Two years. How did I go without this for two years?

"Natalie." He said her name differently when they were in bed together, like it was a gift he was so lucky to have.

He grasped the base of his cock and pulled out. Before he headed to the washroom, he pressed a kiss to her forehead.

She rolled onto her stomach. Her body felt…almost new. She was aware of it in a different way from usual, aware of how she could use it with a man.

She'd nearly forgotten.

Connor came back a minute later and pulled up the covers around them. He slung an arm around her, and she turned her head toward him.

"So," he said.

"So," she echoed.

"Do you want me to pick up your suitcase now?"

Suitcase? What was he talking about?

Then she remembered. It was at her parents' house, where she was supposed to be sleeping tonight. Her parents were getting divorced.

Yet that seemed so far away now. She and Connor were cocooned in this room together, and nothing else could touch them, not tonight.

Connor. She was doing all of this with Connor. It should be hard to wrap her mind around that, but somehow, it wasn't. Everything was simple right now. She'd just had sex and she felt blissed out, and that was all that mattered.

"No," she said. "We'll get the suitcase in the morning."

He continued to look at her in the dim light, stroking her cheek with the pad of his thumb, and it made her feel…cherished, somehow. Something she wasn't used to feeling.

After pressing a kiss to her lips, he turned off the lamp, and she fell asleep with her head on his shoulder.

$$[\ 10\ ]$$

Natalie opened her eyes. The goddamn birds were chirping outside the window, and sunshine was streaming into the room. Had she forgotten to close the curtains last night? And why was she naked?

She sat up with a jolt. She wasn't in her childhood bedroom, but at the bed and breakfast.

In Connor's room.

She'd slept with Connor last night.

He wasn't in bed with her now, but water was running in the washroom. He must be in the shower.

Okay. This was okay. She'd had sex last night. With her friend, which might complicate matters, but she couldn't deny that it had been good sex, and it was exactly what she'd needed after Aunt Louisa had dropped that bombshell. She and Connor would go on like they always had. They'd put this behind them, pretend it hadn't happened. She could do that. Now that it was daylight, she wouldn't find him irresistibly attractive like she had last night, when she was in a weird state of mind.

The door to the washroom opened. Connor stepped out, a towel around his waist.

Maybe this wasn't okay.

Because she still found Connor Douglas really fucking attractive, especially when his broad chest was bare and he was wearing nothing but a towel. She followed the trail of hair below his navel, down, down, down…

Get a grip. She sat up and pulled the sheet over her breasts, a little self-conscious.

"Hey, you," he said.

This was Connor. She shouldn't be feeling this way. He was just a friend. She'd known him for more than fifteen years without having such thoughts about him.

But her skin tingled as he sat next to her on the bed.

"Sleep well?" he asked.

"Put on a damn shirt!"

His lips curved upward and crinkles appeared at the corners of his eyes. He had a very nice smile.

"What's the problem?" he asked, gesturing to his chest. "You liked it last night."

Her cheeks flamed.

Jesus. She couldn't believe they were talking like this. And yet it had felt so simple and *right* yesterday.

He chuckled and flicked his finger under her chin before getting up and putting on a shirt.

Thank God. That was better. Except he sure filled out that T-shirt nicely…

"My suitcase," she said.

He didn't reply immediately, just dropped the towel to the ground before reaching for a pair of boxers.

Apparently, they weren't shy around each other anymore.

She should look away. She really should. But she couldn't help remembering how hard he'd been for her. Could she get him that hard right now? She bet she could. And then…

She swallowed. "My suitcase is at my parents' house. Could you get it for me? I don't want to leave the room in a wrinkled bridesmaid dress."

He pulled on his jeans. "That's my plan. Get your suitcase, and then we can go down to breakfast."

"Sounds good. My dad's always up by eight, so it shouldn't be a problem."

He gave her a kiss on the cheek before heading out the door.

Would things would ever be the same between them again?

When Connor had woken up and seen Natalie asleep beside him, her hair going every which way, he'd thought she was just as beautiful as she'd been the night before, and she was adorably flustered when he came out of the shower. So unlike her.

Hmm.

He drove the short distance to Howard and Judy's house, and he exchanged a few words with Howard about the weather before the older man went upstairs to retrieve the suitcase.

When Connor returned to the bed and breakfast, Natalie was out of the shower. She had a towel wrapped around her, and she was combing her hair.

"Breakfast is really good here," he said to fill the silence. "Yesterday they had ham and cheese soufflés. Since the room is for two guests, it shouldn't be a problem that you're eating with me today, even though you weren't here the first night."

"Right," she said, concentrating very hard on her hair.

"We're okay, aren't we?" He hoped they were okay, and he hoped she'd be interested in another round after they'd gotten some sustenance.

He couldn't remember the last time he'd had such a good time in bed with a woman. He'd slept with a few women since his divorce, but not for a while now, and he hadn't stayed the night those times. But he would have wanted to spend the whole night with Natalie even if they hadn't already arranged to share his room. He'd liked going to sleep with her head on his shoulder.

Interesting.

"We're fine," she said, pulling her clothes out of her suitcase. She went to the washroom and closed the door.

So she wasn't going to undress in front of him.

Well, that was unfortunate.

When Connor and Natalie went downstairs for breakfast, Seth and Simon were seated at a table for four by the window. Simon waved them over.

"How are you two after yesterday's exciting events?" he asked.

Natalie sat down beside Seth, and Connor sat beside Simon.

"I'm wonderful," Natalie said, with more than a hint of sarcasm in her voice. "Just wonderful. Where's the coffee?"

"On the sideboard." Seth pointed to the left.

Connor jumped up to get coffee for the two of them. He knew how Natalie liked hers: a moderate amount of sugar and just a splash of cream. He placed her coffee in front of her and she smiled at him, which sent a pleasant hum through his body.

He took a seat and turned toward Seth and Simon. "What did you two get up to last night after we left?"

"Never mind that," Simon said, leaning toward him. "What did you and Natalie do?"

"Simon," Seth said, "you promised you wouldn't say anything."

"Speaking of that, where's my five dollars? We made a bet, remember?"

Seth glared at him.

Simon looked at the rest of the table. "It was a very simple bet. Before we left the room this morning, I bet Seth that you two would come down to breakfast together."

Connor choked on his coffee. So did Natalie. At exactly the same time, as though they'd choreographed it.

Simon held out his hand. "Five dollars."

Seth rolled his eyes and deposited a five-dollar bill in his husband's hand. Simon kissed him on the cheek.

"I don't want you to get the wrong idea…" Natalie began.

"The wrong idea?" Simon tilted his head. "I have no idea what you're talking about. Please, enlighten me."

She gave him a look. "I didn't want to stay at Mom and Dad's last night because I figured there'd be a fight to rival the *Baffin Island mist* one, and I wouldn't sleep a wink."

So she was going to pretend nothing had happened last night. This caused Connor a touch of disappointment, but he understood.

"What on earth is *Baffin Island mist*?" Simon asked.

"It's a paint color," Seth said. "Our parents argued about what color to paint the living room for a full week. It was awful."

"And yet," Natalie said, "when it came down to it, I always thought they were happy together. But sometimes you can't see what you don't want to see."

A middle-aged woman wearing an apron approached the table. Macy was one of the owners of the bed and breakfast. "What can I get the four of you this morning? There are two options today. Blueberry pancakes and bacon, or spinach omelet."

"Pancakes," Natalie said.

"Pancakes," Connor said.

"My God." Simon looked at Natalie, then Connor. "You're already connected at the mind."

"Stop it," Seth said. "There are only two options, and clearly pancakes and bacon is the sensible choice." He turned to Macy. "I'll have pancakes, too."

"I," Simon began, lifting his nose in the air, "will have the spinach omelet. That's the healthier choice."

"Three pancakes and one omelet," Macy said. "Coming right up."

When she left, Simon turned to Seth and said, "I don't know why you have a problem with Natalie and Connor being together. He seems perfectly nice, and it's been years since Natalie brought anyone home, hasn't it?"

Connor tried to remember her past boyfriends. Which one might she have brought back to Mosquito Bay?

"Just to be clear," Natalie said, "Connor and I are not together. A straight man and woman can sleep in the same room without anything happening."

"That's true, that's true," Simon said, nodding his head. "Very good point, Natalie. But even though you're a bit grumpy—as you usually are in the morning—you have a healthy glow about you, despite everything that happened yesterday."

Natalie contorted her face in an odd way, as though trying to get rid of her healthy glow. Connor stifled a laugh.

Simon was right. She did look good this morning, even when her face was all pinched up.

"I do not have a *healthy glow*," she insisted.

"Oh, but you do," Simon said. "Don't you think so, Seth?"

Seth was looking out the window. He merely grunted.

Simon sighed. "He's in a bad mood because he heard you two having sex last night."

"*What?*" Connor and Natalie said at the same time.

"Apparently, hearing your sister having sex is a very horrible thing. I don't have any siblings, so I wouldn't know."

"I'm not sure why I'm asking," Natalie said, "but what, exactly, did you hear?"

"Nothing." Seth scowled. "We heard nothing."

"You're so charming, husband of mine." Simon reached over and patted his hand. "We didn't hear much, to be honest, and we were both high at the time. But when we were in the hallway, fumbling with our keys, we heard Natalie cry out from the room next door, as well as a few creaks of the bedsprings. Nothing more."

"Dear God." Natalie covered her face with her hands. "I'm going back to the room."

When she started to stand up, Connor reached for her wrist and pulled her back down. "Now, now, after all the work you did last night, you need a good meal." He couldn't resist teasing her.

"You were on top the whole time, so…" She clamped her hand over her mouth as she realized what she'd said.

Simon slapped the table and laughed.

Seth, on the other hand, did not look amused.

Natalie sat back down. "I'm only staying because there's bacon. If there wasn't bacon, I'd already be upstairs."

"Anyway," Simon continued, "we knew you were staying with Connor last night, and we knew there was some, shall we say, *hanky-panky*—"

"No, we shall not say that," Seth grumbled.

"—so it was just a question of whether you'd actually make an appearance at breakfast this morning. Seth figured you wouldn't risk running into us, but I knew otherwise, and now I'm the proud owner of a crisp five-dollar bill." Simon pulled the bill out of his pocket and held it up.

"I thought this weekend couldn't get any worse," Natalie muttered. "Wow, was I wrong."

"Oh, come on, it hasn't been that bad," Simon said. "Sure, your parents are getting divorced, but you had good sex last night, didn't you? It certainly sounded like you were enjoying it… Why Natalie, are you blushing? I've never seen you blush before."

As entertaining as this was, Connor figured he'd better put an end to Natalie's misery. "Simon, you said something about getting high last night?"

"Much better," Seth said. "We'll talk about drugs instead."

"We indulged in some of Iris's weed," Simon said. "Man, she sure can roll a good joint."

They stopped talking as Macy approached with four plates of food. She set the omelet in front of Simon and pancakes in front of everyone else.

"Thank you. This looks delicious." Simon snagged a slice of bacon off Seth's plate.

"Hey!" Seth glared at his husband. "If you wanted bacon, you should have ordered the pancakes. No stealing my food."

"I can't imagine you'll finish that, not after all the Cheetos you ate last night."

"Cheetos?" Natalie perked up. "There were Cheetos? Why didn't I get any?"

Her enthusiasm for Cheetos was rather cute. Connor recalled the last time they'd gone cross-country skiing together and how she'd used chopsticks to eat her post-skiing Cheetos. Now it was easy to imagine himself feeding her Cheetos and then kissing her.

"After we smoked up," Simon said, "Seth insisted we stop at the gas station to get some. We still had half a bag left when we got back to the room. I didn't think you'd be interested, however, seeing as you seemed to have better things to do, what with all the moaning and—"

"Thank you," Natalie said. "I know exactly where this is going. *Again.*"

He laughed. "Alas, I think Seth finished the rest of the bag before we went to sleep."

"You have a terrible memory," Seth said. "You're the one who finished the bag."

"Did not," Simon protested.

Seth rolled his eyes. "Yeah, sure. Say whatever you want, but that doesn't make it true. There were still Cheetos left when I went to bed."

"Crumbs! Orange cheese dust! Not actual Cheetos."

"That's not how I remember it."

"You two argue all the time," Natalie said.

"We do," Simon said. "Next thing you know, we'll be getting a divorce."

Seth shook his head. "That's not funny right now."

Simon began cutting into his omelet. "Don't worry, Natalie. This is all happy bickering. We're not getting divorced. It's our tenth anniversary in September."

"Congratulations," Connor said.

"Thank you. We're planning to go to Spain."

They were quiet for a minute as they focused on their food. The pancakes were indeed delicious, as was the bacon—how could you go wrong with bacon?—and Connor certainly had an appetite after last night. He knocked his foot against Natalie's under the table, and when she smiled at him, warmth bloomed in his chest.

"We're supposed to go to Mom and Dad's for brunch tomorrow," Seth said, "and watch Rebecca open her gifts. Do you think that's still happening?"

"I don't know." Natalie sighed. "I assume something will happen, but maybe just one of them will be there."

"Thanksgiving, Christmas, Easter—what will we do now?"

"I feel stupid worrying about such things, but I can't help it. Everything has always been the same—Mom and Dad together in Mosquito Bay. It doesn't make a big difference in my day-to-day life, but it was nice."

Simon nodded sympathetically. "We only come to Mosquito Bay once or twice a year, but your family…they really are my family. I'm lucky to have such great in-laws." He reached across the table and squeezed Seth's hand, then surreptitiously reached for the bacon. Seth hit his hand out of the way before he could snag any.

"We're glad to have you, too," Natalie said, which seemed uncharacteristically sentimental of her.

Simon turned to Connor. "I don't have any family in Canada aside from my parents, and they weren't happy when I told them

I was gay." He released an unsteady breath. "At first, they refused to come to our wedding, but Ngin Ngin called my mother, and they had a long, loud argument in Cantonese. Ngin Ngin told her how she'd always regretted not going to her son's wedding and convinced her to come, promising we'd have a banquet at a Chinese restaurant."

"Ngin Ngin was uncomfortable with me marrying a man at first, too," Seth said, "but she fell in love with Simon."

"Of course," Simon said. "Because who wouldn't fall in love with me?" He and Seth shared a smile. "My parents still haven't gotten used to the fact that I married a man, but your parents have always been supportive. Your white grandmother and Dennis, however—I could do without them. And Louisa always causes a scene."

"I wish Rebecca hadn't invited them," Seth said.

"Same," Natalie agreed. "But you know Rebecca. She wants everyone to get along. She would hate the drama of not inviting a few family members to her wedding."

"Speaking of Rebecca…" Simon looked at his watch. "It's nine o'clock. Do you think she'll make it down to breakfast? Or do you think she has better things to do upstairs? I'm pretty sure the Superior room has a Jacuzzi and—"

"Stop it." Seth gritted his teeth. "Haven't we been over this already? I don't want to think about my sisters having sex. Not Natalie, and not Rebecca."

Natalie's cheeks flushed. She sent Simon a glare, though it seemed like she was trying to hold back a smile.

Connor couldn't help touching her hand. "You're adorable."

"Aw," Simon said, pressing a hand to his heart.

"When was the last time someone called Natalie adorable?" Seth asked. "I'm not sure it's happened before. Personally, I'm more likely to go with 'cranky' or 'pain in my ass' when describing my sister."

Natalie stuck her tongue out at him.

Connor was getting himself a second cup of coffee when Iris and Ngin Ngin walked into the breakfast room and sat down at the table next to theirs.

"Natalie," Ngin Ngin said. "Why are you here? You weren't here yesterday." Her face lit up. "Ah. You stayed with Connor last night, not with parents. Very good. You trying to make a baby?"

"Ngin Ngin!" Natalie groaned. "Please."

"You're so much fun to tease," Ngin Ngin said. "When you were a little girl, I didn't see you much. Plus, very little English. But now, I make jokes!"

Natalie looked like she wanted to sink into the floor.

Iris grabbed a cup of coffee then came back to the table. "Ngin Ngin, you want coffee?"

She shook her head. "Want to sleep in car. Won't sleep if I have coffee."

"Good idea. I don't need you bugging me about my drug habit on the drive to Toronto."

"You're going back to Toronto today?" Connor asked.

"You have a drug habit?" Seth asked.

"We're heading back as soon as we finish breakfast," Iris said. "Don't worry, I'm not a drug addict. Ngin Ngin is just disturbed that I smoked pot last night. I told her I do it about once a month, and she was aghast."

"Men don't want women who are drug addicts." Ngin Ngin pointed her finger at Iris. "Now you are the last grandchild without boyfriend or husband. I will focus all attention on *you.*"

"I can't wait," Iris muttered.

"What about me?" Natalie asked. "Connor is just a friend."

He couldn't help feeling a flicker of disappointment at those words, even though he'd heard them many times before.

"I don't believe you." Ngin Ngin shook her head. "You are more than friends, and I'm happy about that. But still upset about Howard. Maybe if I went to his wedding, if I approved of Judy from the beginning, he would have happier marriage?"

"Don't blame yourself," Natalie said. "That was forty years ago. You've been supportive for a long time."

"I like Judy. She's a good daughter-in-law. But Judy's mother?" Ngin Ngin shook her head. "Awful woman. And Louisa? She drinks too much." She turned to Iris. "You see? Men don't want women with drug problems. That's why Louisa has three divorces."

"But she got three men to marry her," Iris pointed out.

"I know. Do not understand."

Natalie drained her coffee then stood up. "Time for us to head upstairs."

Simon imitated the noise of bedsprings squeaking, and she rolled her eyes.

"See you soon," she said to Seth and Simon before hugging Ngin Ngin and Iris. "Have a good trip back to Toronto."

Back in the room, Natalie gasped as Connor pressed her against the door and kissed her. Her arms wound around his neck, and she kissed him back. She couldn't help it. God, he tasted good—maple syrup and bacon—and she loved the feel of his body around hers.

He tried to make the sound of bedsprings squeaking, though he wasn't quite as good at it as Simon.

She chuckled. "I can't believe they heard us."

"You know what I realized at breakfast?"

"I'm almost scared to find out."

"You're cute when you're pissed off." He never would have said that to her before. "When everyone was teasing you about me…" Instead of finishing that thought, he covered her mouth with his and slipped his tongue between her lips.

Yeah, she really liked this kissing business. But…

"I should be going," she said.

"Where?"

"To see my friend Kara. I told you about that on the drive down, remember? You're welcome to come with me, but you should be warned: she has three children, ages two, three, and five."

"I'll stay here. Maybe walk around town, see the sights."

She was relieved he didn't want to go with her, actually. Some time apart would probably be good after what happened last night. It would help her get her head on straight.

"Sure," she said. "We can meet up later in the afternoon."

He gave her a kiss on the cheek before she walked out the door, and the feel of his lips on her skin lingered for a long time afterward.

$$[\; 11 \;]$$

KARA'S TWO-YEAR-OLD daughter was throwing her sippy cup around and had yogurt smeared all over her face. She kept trying to smell—or was it kiss?—the golden retriever's ass. Literally kiss its ass.

"She sees dogs sniffing each other's asses, and she gets ideas," Kara said to Natalie.

"Doggie's ass!" said the two-year-old.

"Mommy said a bad word." Kara pulled her youngest child toward her and wiped her face with a paper towel. "Doggie's *bum.*"

The two-year-old ran around the den, screaming, "Doggie's bum! Doggie's bum!" The three-year-old joined in a moment later.

Natalie was sitting on the couch beside Kara, and she could feel a headache coming on.

The idea of having three children under the age of six was positively terrifying. And why would anyone want to bring so many children into this godforsaken world? The place was going to shit. You only had to read the comments section on any news article to know that.

Then there was climate change, which had somehow become a political issue that you believed in or didn't believe in. Many people didn't care what the experts thought, didn't care about scientists' analyses of the data. If there was a snowstorm in April, they considered it proof the planet wasn't warming up.

Natalie was one of the experts, and she was very worried about the state of the world.

Of course, she couldn't wax poetic about the good old days, either. If she'd been born a hundred years ago, her life would hardly have been easy. For starters, she wouldn't have been able to vote. Although women were given the right to vote in 1919, that wasn't *all* women. Chinese Canadians didn't get the right to vote until nearly thirty years later, and while Rebecca might be able to pass as a white woman, Natalie could not.

It was probably for the best that she'd been born when she was. She'd had lots of opportunities. But that didn't mean the world was a great place.

If you were a mother, people attacked you for working, and they attacked you for not working. They attacked you for breastfeeding in public, and they attacked you for not breastfeeding at all, even if it was impossible for you to breastfeed. They complained about child obesity rates, yet they called the cops if they saw two eight-year-olds walking home without an adult. You were under so much pressure to do everything perfectly. People judged your every move.

And if you weren't a mother, everyone was constantly asking when you would become one. Like her extended family at Rebecca's wedding, pointing out that she was getting old.

Kara didn't ask, though, because she was a friend and she knew Natalie's feelings on having children.

"Are you seeing anyone?" she asked instead.

"No."

Kara's eyebrows shot up. "You hesitated."

"I did not." But Natalie might have. Just a little.

"Come on," Kara said, sliding closer to her on the couch.

Natalie glanced at the children. The five-year-old boy was building something out of Duplo, and the two girls were chasing each other. She felt a little weird talking about this when there were three kids in the room, but she decided to tell the truth. "The guy I brought to Rebecca's wedding. We, um, hooked up. It didn't mean anything, though. I was just in a weird place after the wedding reception."

She was brushing it off as though it were no big deal, but it kind of *was* a big deal.

"You and your exciting single life." Kara sighed, then pulled her three-year-old daughter into her arms and tickled the bottom of her feet. "But I wouldn't give this up for the world."

That's what parents always said. Natalie believed her friend truly meant it, even if Kara might wish for a day off to go to the spa, where she would inevitably worry about how her three screaming munchkins were behaving for her husband.

Sometimes, however, Natalie felt like parents said that more to convince themselves than anything else. You couldn't say you wished you didn't have kids, especially right in front of them. Plus, it seemed like some people had children because it was just one of those things you did. They wanted to fit in. Which seemed like a terrible reason to have a child, but Natalie kind of understood. When you got to your mid-thirties and nearly everyone you knew was popping out babies, you started to feel left out if you were childless.

She believed Rebecca really did want children, but she hoped her sister would wait until she and Elliot had been married for a couple of years. They'd gotten married after nine months. Nine months was nothing. And she was only twenty-five years old! That seemed too young to be sure of what you wanted.

Of course, their parents had had children when they were that age.

And look how well that had turned out.

"Is the news about Rebecca's wedding all over town?" Natalie asked.

"Our next-door neighbor rushed over to tell me just before you got here. According to her, one of your grandmothers whacked the other on the head with a cane and she started bleeding, but I'm guessing that's an exaggeration?"

Natalie chuckled. "Ngin Ngin did lunge toward Grandma with a cane over her head, but my brother pulled her back."

"The gossips in town aren't overly concerned with getting the details right."

"No, they are not."

"So," Kara said, "tell me more about the guy you hooked up with."

"We're just friends." It felt like a lie, but it was the truth. "You know Connor? I'm sure I've mentioned him before. He—"

"You slept with *Connor*? You guys have been friends for ages. Was he good?"

Natalie's face heated. "He—"

"Mommy, what are you talking about?" the three-year-old asked.

"Grown-up stuff," Kara said.

"Mommy, I'm hungry."

"Okay, sweetie. I'll start making the frittata." Kara stood up and turned to Natalie. "It'll be nice to cook for someone who appreciates real food. I even bought arugula."

Natalie got on the floor with the children.

"What are you making?" she asked the five-year-old, gesturing at the Duplo.

"A stable for my unicorn." He held up a white-and-yellow stuffed unicorn that looked well-loved.

"Natalie!" The three-year-old tapped her shoulder. "Will you make me a crown?" She held up a sheet of yellow construction paper.

"Sure," Natalie said. "Do you want to be a princess?"

The three-year-old shook her head solemnly. "I want to be a queen. Queens are more powerful."

"I want a crown!" The two-year-old rushed over. "I want to be a princess!"

"If you get me another sheet of paper, I'll make you each a crown."

Natalie spent the next fifteen minutes cutting out and taping two crowns. The little girls were thrilled when they each got a crown placed on their heads. Then the golden retriever started eating the two-year-old's crown, and Natalie had to make a third one.

She could enjoy this for a few hours. But she didn't want it to be her life.

After leaving Kara's, Natalie went to her parents' house and rang the doorbell, feeling a little guilty that she hadn't stayed here last night.

Dad answered.

"Is it just you?" she asked.

He nodded.

She wasn't surprised. She hadn't expected them both to be home.

Her parents together? That was a thing of the past.

She followed her father into the living room, where presents wrapped in white and pink and silver paper covered the coffee table. Standing up against the far wall was an oil painting of a garden. Natalie walked over to examine it.

"Where did this come from?" she asked.

"Bernard," Dad said, a touch of bitterness in his voice. "He paints, you see, in addition to being a successful businessman. Judy was going to say she bought it at an art fair when she gave it to Rebecca, but now…" He shrugged. "No use lying."

"Are you jealous of Bernard?"

A foolish hope sprang up in her chest. Her father could win her mother back with a grand romantic gesture!

Jesus, what was wrong with her?

"Jealousy is not what I would call it," Dad said.

"Have you met him?"

"No." Dad put his hand on her shoulder and continued to look at the painting. "It wasn't so much that we didn't want to deal with our mothers' reactions, but even before Rebecca announced she was getting married, we didn't want to disappoint her."

"What about me and Seth?"

"You've been world-weary since you were a child. You can cope with anything."

"Thanks, Dad."

He turned toward her. "Seth will be fine. He always is. Rebecca, however... She'll be fine, too, I guess. I hate that it ruined her wedding, though." He shook his head. "Dammit. I never liked Louisa."

"She's always been a bit much."

"I put up with her because she was the only one who stood by your mother when we got married. But she's a borderline alcoholic who can't commit to anything."

They stood in silence for a moment.

"Mom has Bernard," Natalie said. "Do you have someone, too?"

"I do not."

"Are we still having brunch tomorrow? Will you both be there?"

"That's the plan." He paused. "You didn't come home last night. Where were you?"

"I stayed at the bed and breakfast with Connor."

"Yet you've been keen to emphasize that he's just your friend, not your boyfriend."

Her mind wandered back to what they'd done last night, to

how he'd kissed her as they'd danced under the stars, then made her soar in bed afterward.

"Just my friend," she repeated.

"As your father, I shall not ask for further details or inquire if the definition of 'friend' has changed since I was young."

Natalie laughed, even though things would never be the same again.

"Mom told me you were making Rebecca's present," she said. "What is it?"

"I'll show you." He motioned for her to follow him down to the basement.

When Rebecca was four, Dad had made her a little table and chair. He'd painted them purple—her favorite color—with stenciled pink hearts and stars. Then he'd built her a matching wooden chest and filled it with construction paper, markers, crayons, and stickers.

When she'd opened her present on Christmas morning, she'd given him the biggest grin in the world.

"Daddy!" she'd cried. "I love you!"

"Your father built it himself," Mom had said.

"Really? It didn't come from the store?"

"No."

"Can you teach me? I want to make something for you!"

God, Rebecca had been cute.

"When you're older," he'd said, and she'd scrunched up her face. He'd brought the table and chair and chest to the den. "Just for my little artist."

Drawing had been her favorite thing to do. For the week after Christmas, every picture she drew—and she did several a day—was for him, half of them of smiling butterflies. Then she'd gotten into a flamingo phase, and it was all flamingos for a while.

She'd given many of those pictures to Natalie, who still had a couple of them.

When Rebecca was older, he did teach her a bit of carpentry. They'd built a bookshelf together, and for Dad's fiftieth birthday, she'd made him a bedside table.

And now, Natalie was looking at the pair of bedside tables that her father had made for Rebecca as her wedding present. They were stained a warm brown.

"They're nice," she said, and then she glanced over at the little purple table and chair, gathering dust in the corner of the basement. She wished she could go back to a simpler time, when Rebecca was small and innocent and her parents were still together. When her father's black hair was not streaked with gray.

Actually, now that she took a closer look, she realized it wasn't just streaked with gray—most of it was gray. Her father was getting old. When had that happened?

She turned toward the storage shelves. The cream-colored box that contained her mother's wedding dress was still there.

Suddenly, she didn't want to be in her childhood home anymore.

Besides, it was time to meet Connor. She'd told him she'd be finished around three o'clock, and it was just about three. She couldn't go back in time, but she could go to Connor. The thought of being in his arms again put a smile on her face, even though she'd panicked when she woke up in his bed this morning.

With Connor, she could let her guard down; she could be herself, and it was okay. She often felt a little on edge, even around people who cared about her, but not with him.

She released a breath. For this weekend, she would just let whatever happened...happen. They could sleep together again, and that would be fine. It would be a lot of fun, in fact. She'd treat the weekend in Mosquito Bay as a break from their regular life.

What happened in Mosquito Bay could stay in Mosquito Bay.

When they returned to Ottawa, it might be a little difficult to return to the way things were before, but she knew they'd stay friends.

She could count on Connor.

[12]

CONNOR SAT BY THE LAKE, his arm slung over the back of the bench. It was the same bench where he and Natalie had sat last night after the reception.

Hard to believe how much had changed in the past twenty-four hours.

His ex-wife hadn't liked Natalie much. Natalie wasn't his only female friend, but she was his only single female friend who wasn't also friends with Sharon. Sharon had trusted Connor, he knew that, but she'd always been a bit suspicious of Natalie. Not that Sharon had had anything to worry about back then.

But now his feelings for Natalie seemed to be evolving. At first, he'd thought it was just sex between friends; now, he wondered if it was more than that.

He kept looking at his phone, waiting for her to text him to say she was leaving Kara's. He couldn't wait to see her again, even though he'd only seen her a few hours ago, and it wasn't just because he wanted to sleep with her, although that would certainly be welcome. He wanted to know how she was. He wanted simple touches, like clasping her hand in his.

A simple touch could mean a whole lot.

Maybe it had something to do with seeing Natalie in her hometown. Seeing her with her family, the people who meant a lot to her. And after all the years he'd heard her talk about her sister, from the time Rebecca had been a child, it was nice to actually meet her.

His phone beeped. It was Natalie, saying she was done and asking where she should meet him. He texted her back.

Ten minutes later, she slid onto the bench beside him with a sigh. He wrapped his arm around her and kissed her cheek.

"How was it?" he asked.

"Oh, it was good. Exhausting, though. When there are three young children, they're never all happy at the same time. Someone's always fussing. But they're cute. I made them crowns. The older girl—she's three—said she wanted to be a queen instead of a princess because queens are more powerful."

He laughed softly, imagining Ariana saying the same thing, but at the same time, he felt an inexplicable sadness.

He shook his head to clear that feeling away.

"Then I went to see my father," she said. "I didn't stay long, but he confirmed that yes, brunch with the whole family is still happening tomorrow. Should be tons of fun."

"Wow, that didn't sound sarcastic at all."

"Who, me? Sarcastic?" She grinned at him, and it sent pleasure coiling through his body.

He never used to feel like this around Natalie. Well, maybe he had when he was eighteen or nineteen, but that felt like a lifetime ago.

"What did you do?" she asked. "Explore the town?"

"Yep. It took me all of twenty minutes."

"That's why I don't come back very often. There's nothing to do, and it's a long way from Ottawa. Plus, it burns a lot of fossil fuel to get here."

He took her hand in his. "It turns me on when you talk about fossil fuel emissions."

"You have a serious problem," she muttered as he bent to kiss behind her ear.

It was the same between them…and yet it was completely different. He was holding her hand and kissing her, and those things were not meaningless.

"Why did your parents settle in Mosquito Bay?" he asked.

"This is where my mom grew up. All of her siblings and her mother still live within half an hour of here. My parents lived in Toronto after they were married, but a year after I was born, they moved back because my mom missed it."

"Your dad grew up in Toronto, right?"

She nodded. "My grandparents had a restaurant on Dundas Street. They came here in the early fifties, a few years after Canada lifted the Chinese Exclusion Act, which had banned Chinese immigrants. They're from southern China."

He'd known Natalie for seventeen years. He knew lots of things about her, but that wasn't enough now. He needed to know everything, including her family history.

"I thought your family spoke Toisanese," he said, "but Simon mentioned Ngin Ngin talking to his parents in Cantonese."

"Toisanese is what they spoke in their village. It's somewhat similar to Cantonese. Many people who speak Toisanese also speak Cantonese, like they speak in Hong Kong, where Simon was born. His family lived in England for a number of years before coming to Canada, if you were wondering about his accent."

"But you don't speak Toisanese or Cantonese."

"I know a few words. Not much. When we were kids, Dad had to translate when Ngin Ngin talked to us because she barely spoke English then, but now her English is pretty good. We can actually hold conversations, which wasn't possible before. She lived and worked in Chinatown, and I think my grandfather discouraged her from having an outside life and taking English classes. Perhaps he didn't want her to be independent. I'm not sure. We don't talk about that."

He laced his fingers with hers, and she didn't pull away.

"Maybe if we'd been on good terms with my father's family when I was little, I would have been interested in learning Toisanese, but the rare times we went to Toronto to see them, I hated it. It was stiff and uncomfortable, and we had to spend a long time in the car." She tucked a strand of hair, which had escaped her ponytail, behind her ear. "I wonder if Dad will leave Mosquito Bay now, maybe go to Toronto so he'll be near Ngin Ngin and Rebecca. And his brother, but they're not close." She shook her head. "Maybe Mom will leave, too, if this Bernard guy lives in Toronto. I saw one of his oil paintings at my parents' house."

"Really?"

"Yeah. He's a pretty good artist. It's a wedding present for Rebecca, and Mom was going to lie about where it was from, but I guess that's not necessary now." She cracked a wry smile.

He squeezed her shoulder.

"There are some things you don't think will ever change, you know? I thought my parents would always stay together and live in that house, and I'd always be able to go back to my childhood home. Now I feel kind of…" She turned her head toward the lake. "Unanchored, I guess. But I'll be fine. Eventually. Dad believes I can cope with anything."

Connor believed that, too, but he didn't want her to have to do it alone.

"What'll we do for the rest of the day?" she asked, her voice a little more upbeat now.

"I made reservations for dinner at six thirty, at a restaurant just out of town."

"Cardinal's?"

He nodded. "I thought we could walk there. A long, leisurely walk along the water, followed by a nice dinner."

She punched him lightly. "That sounds kind of romantic, Connor."

Yeah, it did.

He liked the idea of a romantic evening with Natalie.

"My first boyfriend took me here for our two-week anniversary," Natalie said after the waitress had taken their orders.

Connor experienced a twinge of jealousy for this man who had been with Natalie two decades ago. She'd mentioned her high-school boyfriend before, but they'd broken up before university, before Connor had met her.

"Two-week anniversary?" Connor repeated, reaching for his glass of wine.

She made a face. "Yeah. Gavin was very sweet. It was a big deal to go here for a date back when we were in high school because it's the most expensive restaurant in Mosquito Bay. Which really isn't saying much, but when we were seventeen, if a guy took you here, it meant he really liked you. And Gavin did really like me. He even wrote me poetry."

"Was it any good?"

"Of course not. He was a seventeen-year-old kid in love for the first time. It was awful, though I was touched by the gesture. What about your first girlfriend?"

"Amanda Cooke. We were together for six weeks and two days back in grade ten, and I never wrote her any poetry. We had a lot of frantic, clumsy make-out sessions, until the day I caught her making out with Mikey Galloway behind the portables."

"I hope you punched him."

"I didn't want to get in trouble, so I just slunk away." He gave Natalie his best puppy-dog face.

She reached over and touched his cheek. "How awful."

"I was in a foul mood for weeks. I even swore off girls."

"How long did that last?"

He shrugged. "About a month. Then Mikey Galloway stole that girl away from me, too."

"Who was this boy? The coolest guy in school?"

"Something like that. He was a real jerk. I think he's in jail now, and I'm sitting in a lovely restaurant on the water, enjoying wine with a beautiful woman."

She managed to blush and roll her eyes at the same time. "Oh, Connor, come on."

"I mean it."

She regarded him for a moment. "I know."

She put her hand on his knee and was just starting to trail her fingers upward when their food arrived. She immediately sat back, ramrod straight, as the waitress placed her eggplant parmesan in front of her.

Connor had ordered the perch, fresh from Lake Huron. It was excellent, though maybe that had more to do with the company than anything else.

They tried each other's food, which made it feel more like a date. He and Natalie wouldn't normally do that when they went out to dinner together. In Ottawa, they'd usually just go to the bar and maybe order a sandwich and fries along with their beer—nothing fancy.

He wouldn't put his hand on top of hers, like he was doing now.

And his gaze wouldn't be drawn to her cleavage.

And they wouldn't share strawberry panna cotta with Florentine cookies for dessert.

He tried to feed her a bite off his spoon, and she gave him a look.

"Really?" she said. "You want to be *that* couple?"

"I didn't think you'd go for it." But he was pleased she'd referred to them as a couple, though she didn't seem to be aware of what she'd said. He had a feeling that if she were, she'd cover her mouth and say she didn't mean it.

"Oh my God. *Natalie.*" The high-pitched female voice burst through the moment, and a woman in a bright sundress hurried over to their table. She looked about their age.

"Alicia," Natalie said, her reaction far more restrained.

"It's so good to see you! It's been years. You're in town for your sister's wedding, I assume? I heard about what happened. Your parents are getting divorced…" Alicia clucked her tongue. "Your mother was always so nice to me. And who's this? Is he your husband? No, he can't be—I would have heard if you were married, even though you don't keep your Facebook profile up to date. Somebody would have told me."

"This is Connor," Natalie said, gesturing toward him. "He's…" Her voice trailed off, and she merely smiled at him.

She didn't insist he was just a friend, but she didn't say anything else, either.

"You guys are so cute!" Alicia gushed. "I've been married…oh, it'll be seven years next week, but knowing Marv, he'll forget our anniversary. We have twins—they're five years old now. They drive me crazy, so I'm having a girls' night out with my sisters." She tilted her head to the other side of the restaurant, toward two women in their thirties. "But I already miss the little dears, even though I desperately need some time away. Do you have children?"

Natalie shook her head. She looked a little stiff.

"We're getting old, aren't we? Not much time left. I think I'm good with the twins, but maybe you want more than two. You were always so good with your sister. Anyway, you should come sit with us after you're done your dessert, and we can catch up some more!"

"Um. It's been good to see you again, Alicia, but we've got plans."

"Of course you do. You and your handsome man. I'll leave you to it!" Alicia bent down and gave Natalie a quick hug, which seemed to catch her off guard, before hurrying off.

"Former classmate?" Connor asked, once she was gone.

Natalie nodded. "I run into her every few years, and she always acts like we used to be the closest of friends, but we never were. She's exhausting. I can take her in five-minute intervals, but if we spend any longer together, I want to hit her over the head with a frying pan."

"You have quite the violent streak."

"I know. I'm charming that way."

"You're certainly charming, especially when you have panna cotta on your lip." He leaned forward. "Want me to lick it off?"

"I'll do the panna cotta-licking honors myself, thank you." Her tongue darted out and licked her top lip. That simple action was so erotic, and his spoon froze on the way to his mouth.

The thought of her tongue on his body…

God, he wanted her.

"So, what are we going to do now?" Natalie asked once they'd left the restaurant. The days were getting longer, and it still wasn't dark.

"We could drive up and down Main Street a couple dozen times?" Connor suggested.

"Um…"

"Or we could find some more alcohol and get plastered?"

"I can see the appeal, but…"

"We could make some herbal tea back at the bed and breakfast and drink it on the rooftop patio as we compose bad poetry for each other. Would you prefer a sonnet or a limerick?"

She burst into laughter.

He kissed her, the taste of that amazing dessert mingling with the taste of *her*, Natalie, the woman he wanted so desperately, even though he'd thought of her as just a friend for years. After he'd forced himself to get over his crush back in university, she'd remained firmly in the friend zone, but now, things were changing.

He wrapped his arms around her and murmured, "Or you could spend the night in my bed."

"I thought you'd never ask."

When they entered the Ontario room, Connor swung Natalie up into his arms. She shrieked in surprise, and he couldn't help but smile.

"Careful," he said. "Seth and Simon might have heard that."

"Oh my God." She covered her mouth with her hand as he carried her to the bed. "I can't believe they heard us last night. Tonight, I'll be quiet."

"Is that a challenge?" he asked, depositing her on the mattress.

She laughed. "Dammit, Connor."

He lay down on top of her and covered her mouth with his, his hands coming up to her cheeks. She tasted so good.

Unlike yesterday, they weren't in formal clothes. No suit that might get wrinkled, no sexy bridesmaid dress, no curls tumbling down Natalie's shoulders—rather, her hair was tied up in a simple ponytail.

He slid his hands under her shirt and lifted it over her head. Next, he removed her bra, and then his hands were on her breasts, his thumb flicking over her brownish-pink nipple as she squirmed against him.

"Touch me *now*," she said.

He grinned. "I'm already touching you."

"You know what I mean."

"Now I'll just make you wait longer."

She rolled her eyes, then closed them when he unbuttoned her jeans and slid his hand inside her panties. He ran his finger along her slit, and her body jumped under his. She struggled with the fastening on his pants before slipping her hand inside and wrapping it around his erection.

After stroking him for a minute, she removed his clothing and straddled his waist, rubbing herself against him before taking his cock in her mouth. There was no preamble, no teasing the tip, no sliding her hand up and down first. She simply took him between her lips, as much as she could manage.

He wouldn't last long with her mouth on him, so he took off the rest of her clothes in a hurry and licked between her legs. She closed a hand over her mouth, struggling to be silent as he ran his tongue around her entrance, then around her clit.

How had they gone so many years without doing this? If he'd known what it would be like with Natalie…

He couldn't wait any longer to be inside her.

"Connor." She shoved at his shoulder.

"Yes, darling." He reached for a condom. "I'm ready."

She patted the pillow. "Lie down."

He did as requested and rolled on the condom. She raised herself above him then slowly eased herself down on his cock, until he was fully seated inside her and surrounded by her heat.

My God. She was exquisite.

She moved up and down on him, and he met her stroke for stroke, his hands cupping her ass. When she lowered her chest to his, he pulled her dark hair out of its elastic and released it so it surrounded his face as she kissed him. Her tongue swept inside his mouth.

It was all too much, and yet it was not enough, and yet it was perfect.

She sped up and buried her face in his shoulder as her orgasm rushed over her. Her cries were muffled, but one day, he wanted to do this in his house, where she could be as loud as she wanted.

He rolled them over so she was underneath him, her hair fanned out on the pillow. He took her with slow, deep strokes, and her shaky breathing gratified him.

When he came inside her, he felt completely undone.

[13]

"Let's go down to the beach," Natalie said.

Connor pressed a kiss to her temple. "It's ten o'clock at night."

Yeah, it was, and they'd just had sex. Natalie didn't understand why she felt the urge to go to the beach, but she felt oddly spontaneous and happy, and she didn't want this feeling to end.

She stood up. "Come on. I used to do this when I was a teenager and there was nothing else to do in Mosquito Bay. I think the bed and breakfast provides beach towels." She went to the closet and pulled two colorful towels down from the top shelf.

"You're not planning on going swimming, are you?"

She gave him a look. "Of course not. It's May. The water is frigid."

They walked down to the beach, and when Connor took her hand, she didn't pull away. It felt nice. He squeezed, and she squeezed back.

They laid out their beach towels on the sand, several meters from the water, and sat down. It was chillier now that the sun had set. She should have brought a sweater.

But then Connor wrapped his arm around her, and that was enough.

She leaned against him and took a few deep breaths of the clean, crisp air. It was quiet out here, with only the sound of water lapping the shore.

All of the crap that had happened this weekend felt far away. She was with Connor, and everything was okay. He made her feel like it would all turn out in the end.

He'd always done that, she realized, but especially this weekend.

"I miss seeing all the stars when we're in Ottawa," she said. "There are never this many in the city, and it's never this quiet."

"Do you miss living here?"

"Not really. I never could have stayed. There are moments like this, though, when it's nice to be in Mosquito Bay. Nice to be away from my regular life."

Nice to be here with you.

Her thoughts were rather mushy right now, and normally, she'd think they were silly and push them aside, but today, she didn't bother.

Connor cupped her cheeks in his hands, as though she was precious and delicate, and kissed her mouth softly, tenderly. Again and again, always coming back for more, and she returned the kiss before resting her head on his shoulder.

They sat there in silence for a few minutes, and then she jumped up. "Let's dance again."

She didn't know what had come over her, but she'd just go with it.

He smiled at her crookedly in the darkness of the night. He stood, taking one of her hands in his and putting his other hand on her waist.

"Don't you dare touch my nipple this time," she said.

"Oh, you mean like this?" He flicked her nipple and grinned at her.

"Connor."

"Natalie."

They moved back and forth together. Then he let go of her waist and spun her in a circle with his other hand, and she laughed in a way she almost never laughed. Like there was nothing holding her back.

When he turned her in a circle for the second time, she tripped in the sand, but he caught her before she could fall and brought her up for another kiss.

"I guess you can't handle my fancy moves," he said as they returned to stepping back and forth.

"It was hardly a *fancy* move." She let go of his shoulder and swatted his chest. "The sand is uneven, that's all, and now I have sand in my shoes."

She was just wearing a T-shirt, jeans, and running shoes. But he looked at her like he had last night. Like she was everything.

How…? Why…?

She wouldn't dwell on it, not now. She would just enjoy it.

They continued to slow dance by the lake. There were countless stars above, countless tiny grains of sand beneath their feet, and the light breeze carried the faint scent of lilacs. And there was the large man holding her hand and smiling fondly down at her.

She had the strangest feeling that this might be the most romantic moment of her life, and she was woefully unprepared for that.

The wind picked up and lifted up the edge of one of the towels, and Natalie jumped away from Connor and threw herself down on the towel so it wouldn't blow away. Connor threw himself onto the other towel.

She laughed again. She felt practically giddy right now.

He drew her toward him and pressed the length of his body against hers as they kissed once more. It was like she was a teenager again, making out on the beach, without a mortgage and a career and insufferable relatives to worry about.

Okay, scratch that. The relatives hadn't changed.

But this…it felt good.

She wrapped her arms more tightly around him; she could feel him getting hard.

"You know what would be really sweet of you," she said.

"I'm listening."

"If you swept me up in your arms and carried me all the way back to the bed and breakfast."

"Is that so?"

He stood up and swept her up in his arms, and she shrieked in delight.

"The towels," she said.

He bent down, allowing her to grab the towels, then started walking across the beach, back toward town.

She couldn't believe it. She was actually being carried like she was some damsel in distress. She'd been joking when she'd said he should carry her back.

Just as she had that thought, he huffed and set her down on her feet.

"You're too heavy," he said.

"Such a sweet thing for you to say."

But the way he smiled at her then…it was everything.

At three in the morning, Natalie woke up to go to the washroom, and when she returned, she spent a while looking at Connor as he slept.

The time she'd spent with him this weekend…somehow it made her feel that maybe, one day, she would always go to sleep next to someone else, always have someone to hug her and kiss her goodnight. Someone who loved her for who she was and wanted to marry her.

Hope. It was an odd feeling.

It was also odd that, only a day after learning her parents were getting divorced, she was already thinking of marriage as something she wanted again.

"Hey," Connor whispered. "You awake?"

In response, she stroked her hand over the scruff on his chin, then smiled sleepily at him before rolling onto her back and closing her eyes.

And before she fell asleep, she had the surprising thought that maybe the person who'd want to marry her would be Connor.

[14]

Cheetos.

That was Natalie's first thought when she woke up the next morning. For some reason, she was craving Cheetos.

She opened her eyes and looked at the man lying next to her. This morning, waking up in Connor's bed didn't make her jolt upright.

He was sleeping on his side, his hands tucked under his head, and he looked…well, cute.

Yeah, she'd just thought of Connor, who must be over two hundred pounds, as *cute*, and suddenly, their late-night trip to the beach came rushing back to her. He'd danced with her and carried her, and he'd caused a strange fluttery feeling in her chest.

Now *that* made her jolt up. What on earth was going on?

She got out of bed and put on yesterday's clothes plus a sweatshirt. Then she made herself some herbal tea—much healthier than Cheetos—and took it up to the rooftop patio. It was still early, and the sun was low on the horizon. She looked down at the quiet streets. No cars were out yet, and the only noise was the birds.

She had a sip of her chamomile tea, which wasn't nearly as satisfying as Cheetos, and turned her thoughts back to Connor.

Yesterday afternoon, she'd decided to treat their weekend in Mosquito Bay as a break from reality. It was supposed to be just sex, but yesterday evening, there had been an intimacy that made it feel like more.

She couldn't start a relationship right now, though, especially not with Connor. She still believed that after a weekend of sex, they could go back to their usual friendship, more or less, but if they started a relationship, that would be different. If it didn't work out, then it would be difficult—impossible, perhaps—to go back to being friends. She valued their friendship, especially now. He'd given up his long weekend to spend fourteen hours in the car with her and attend her sister's wedding—that wasn't the kind of friend you found every day. They'd known each other for years. It wasn't something she wanted to risk losing.

And yet last night, at three in the morning, she'd felt like maybe it could work out for her after all, maybe even with Connor.

That feeling of hope?

It freaked the fuck out of her.

Now that she was thinking clearly again, her hope was fading, and she could see that a relationship with him probably wouldn't end well. Sure, maybe the first few weeks would be fun, but at some point, they would have that awkward conversation, the one that had been the downfall of every single one of her relationships in the past six years.

Do you want children?

Natalie was pretty sure Connor did.

Unlike many of the men she'd dated, she knew he wouldn't judge her for not wanting kids. However, if he wanted children of his own, they were not compatible.

Now, there was a chance he didn't. Very unlikely, given her past experience. The men she dated always wanted them.

But even in the unlikely event that he was different from all those men, it was hard to imagine they could make it when her own parents, who'd had to defy their families to get married, were splitting up. Even before her parents' secret had been revealed, she hadn't really believed in lasting love for herself, and she'd made it to thirty-six without a marriage proposal.

Well, that wasn't quite true. Anthony had said he would marry her *if* she didn't terminate the pregnancy—did that count as a proposal?

Natalie put down her cup of tea and shook her head to rid it of that awful memory.

Dammit. She really needed those Cheetos.

When Connor woke up at eight thirty, he experienced a moment of panic when Natalie was nowhere to be found. He grabbed his phone to text her and noticed he'd missed a phone call yesterday evening—he'd been so caught up with Natalie that he hadn't once checked his phone, hadn't picked up when Sharon had called.

First, he texted Natalie. *Where are you?*

She replied immediately. *I'm on the roof. Will be down soon.*

He let out the breath he'd been holding. He hadn't really been worried about her, but it was good to know where she was.

Last night had been…lovely. The walk, the dinner, the dancing on the beach. And the sex, of course. It had felt like they were a real couple, which was interesting.

He pushed that thought aside. It was time to call his ex-wife.

He was on decent terms with Sharon. It had been a relatively amicable separation, as far as these things went. They didn't talk very often now, however, and seeing his ex-wife's name on his phone made him fear that something bad had happened.

He called her number, and as soon as he heard the first ring, he realized he was naked. There was something weird about having a phone conversation when you were naked, even though the other person couldn't see you, and it was especially weird when you were calling your ex.

He was about to end the call and put on some clothes when she picked up.

"Connor!" She sounded pleased to hear from him, which was not what he'd expected.

"You called?"

"I have something to tell you. I wanted you to hear it from me, rather than online."

"What is it?" he asked, his voice a bit strained.

"I'm pregnant."

Once, that would have caused more complicated emotions, but now, he was simply happy for her. "Congratulations. How far along?"

"Sixteen weeks. I've told my family and close friends, but I'm going to put it on Facebook, and I just wanted to tell you first."

There was something else he wanted to know. He couldn't help it.

Sharon told him without him having to ask. "My boyfriend and I have been together for eight months, and I moved in with him after I found out. We're planning to get married before the baby comes, just at City Hall."

So there was a boyfriend. A boyfriend and a baby-to-be.

He was genuinely happy for her. It was what she'd always wanted, and he wished only good things for her. He'd felt terribly guilty when he'd asked for the divorce, guilty that he wasn't willing to give her the life she'd wanted, guilty that she'd squandered so many years on him before he realized they didn't want the same thing. Guilty that he'd fallen out of love.

But now, he felt lighter. The tension in his chest uncoiled.

She was going to have what she'd always wanted.

Underneath those positive feelings, however, he felt a bit of unease. Even jealousy, if he was honest with himself. He wasn't jealous of her new boyfriend, but jealous that she had what she wanted…and he didn't.

But what did he want?

Natalie.

The answer came to him immediately. He wanted more than a couple stolen nights in her hometown. He wanted more than the occasional beer on a Saturday night, or an afternoon skiing or hiking in the woods. He wanted a serious relationship, and Sharon's news somehow felt like permission for him to fully move on.

If it were anyone other than Natalie, though, he wouldn't be thinking about a relationship right now. The women he'd dated casually since his divorce…he'd felt bored when he was with them. But he'd known Natalie for many years, and he knew he'd never feel that way with her.

She was special.

The thought of her made him smile, but he didn't let himself hope too much. He'd never been particularly good at revealing his feelings; besides, he'd likely have some of the same problems he'd had with Sharon. He hated to think of it, but it was true.

"Connor?" Sharon said.

"I'm glad it worked out for you," he said. "Really, I am. But I'm out of town for a wedding, and I've got to go."

He ended the call and padded across the room to the bathroom. He was about to open the door when Natalie came into the room. Her lips curved when she saw him, and her gaze dipped to his crotch.

Ah, yes. He was still naked.

She sauntered over to him and put a hand on his bicep, then suddenly jerked back.

"Shit," she said. "I forgot I had Cheeto dust all over my hands."

"You were eating Cheetos first thing in the morning?"

"Herbal tea didn't satisfy me, so I went to the gas station and bought a bag. Damn Seth for putting the idea in my head. Unfortunately, I didn't have chopsticks, so now my hands are a mess."

He raised her hand to his mouth and sucked on one of her fingers. "What's wrong with Cheeto fingers? Rather tasty, in my opinion."

In response, she rubbed her hands down his chest, smearing Cheeto dust everywhere.

He laughed. "Good thing I was about to shower. You're welcome to join me, of course."

"Mm, I'm not going to say no to that." She started to reach for the bottom of her T-shirt then stopped. "You're going to have to take off my shirt or it'll get orange, too."

"Gladly."

In the last thirty minutes, Natalie had somehow managed to shower, have sex with Connor, pack up her suitcase, and make out with Connor. Really, it was astonishing how much she could accomplish when she put her mind to it. If only she was always that productive.

Now they sat in the breakfast room with Seth and Simon. After demolishing a bag of Cheetos, Natalie didn't need breakfast. Besides, they were having brunch at her parents' house in an hour. But coffee was more than welcome, and she was on her second cup.

Connor and Seth, however, were eating sausage and scrambled eggs.

"He eats like a tank," Simon said, slapping his husband on the shoulder. "And not only when he smokes pot."

"He's been that way since he was thirteen," Natalie muttered, then took a sip of her coffee.

She should be in a better mood. She'd just had sex, after all. But her weekend with Connor was almost over and she wished she could have something more with him, though she knew it was an impossibility.

"How was your night?" Simon asked, waggling his eyebrows. "Get up to any trouble?"

Seth glared at him.

"What?" Simon said in a perfectly pleasant voice. "Don't you want me to be friendly with your family?"

"We talked about this," Seth grumbled. "You are not allowed to talk to Natalie about what she did last night. I'm quite sure I don't want to know."

Simon regarded Natalie. "Hmm. She seems a little too grouchy to have had sex…or maybe she's grouchy because she was up all night due to a sex marathon. Yes, I bet that's it."

"Who's having a sex marathon?"

Natalie whipped her head around at the sound of her sister's voice. Rebecca and Elliot were standing beside their table, Rebecca wearing jeans and a blouse and looking like a happily married young woman.

"Ignore Simon," Natalie said. "He's just joking around."

"Oh my God!" Rebecca put her hands to her mouth. "You and Connor! I thought you said you were just friends. This is the *best* news."

"Don't you dare tell Mom and Dad."

"Please do." Simon folded his hands behind his head and leaned back in the chair. "Mind you, it won't be as entertaining without your extended family there."

"Why does everyone care about my sex life?" Natalie asked.

"I just want you to be happy!" Rebecca grinned and took Natalie's hands in hers.

Natalie couldn't help but smile back at her sister.

"Why are you guys eating breakfast?" Rebecca gestured toward Connor and Seth.

"The food is delicious here," Seth said. "Didn't want to miss it, since we paid for it."

"Seth is always hungry," Simon said. "And maybe Connor is, too, or he's still recovering from the aforementioned sex marathon."

Connor winked at Natalie, and dammit, that was enough to make her think of all the fun they'd had in the shower. She already wanted to do it again, even though she'd had an orgasm less than an hour ago. This man was wreaking havoc on her body.

But you can't have him. Not really.

She couldn't let herself forget that.

Once they returned to Ottawa, they should stop sleeping together. She still thought it was best if they just treated this as a weekend that was separate from reality. After all, it had involved her grandmothers nearly beating each other with canes—it was hardly an ordinary weekend. That spark of something more would disappear when she left Mosquito Bay, wouldn't it?

It better. She couldn't pursue a relationship with him. There was no point in saying anything when it would never work out between them.

Hope was a dangerous thing, and somehow, despite everything that had happened this weekend, Connor had given her a spark of hope.

That bastard.

That kind, caring, dependable bastard.

"I talked to Sharon while you were eating Cheetos on the roof," Connor said as he drove away from the bed and breakfast.

The mention of his ex-wife irritated Natalie. She didn't want to hear about another woman he'd slept with.

She'd always liked Sharon just fine, though, and had been surprised when Connor told her they were getting divorced.

"Do you talk to her often?" she asked.

"No. We get along well enough, but we see no reason to stay in each other's lives." He kept his eyes on the road. "She's got a boyfriend now. They've been together for a while, and she called to tell me she's pregnant. I guess she decided it wasn't the sort of thing I should find out via Facebook." He paused. "I'm glad she's getting what she wants. She always wanted a few kids."

What about you? Do you want kids? She opened her mouth to ask him the question, but all that came out was a squeak. She couldn't do it.

A tiny part of her was holding on to the fantasy of them being a couple, and she couldn't ruin it by reality. After all, she was pretty sure he wanted kids, but as long as she didn't ask, she had that blasted spark of hope. Besides, she expected these feelings to go away soon, so there was no point in learning the truth.

Dating had been different when she'd first met Connor. She'd been eighteen, and going out with boys had just been about having fun. There wasn't the level of baggage that there was at thirty-six, the concern about the future. Nobody feared they were running out of time. At eighteen, dating had seemed so simple, and she'd been surrounded by people her age at university.

Once, when she was older, she'd been in Sharon's position. When Natalie was thirty-two and had been with Anthony for six months, she'd gotten pregnant, even though they'd always used birth control. She'd been pissed off when she saw the results of the home pregnancy test. Then she'd told Anthony, because wasn't it reasonable that one of the first things she did was tell the man who'd knocked her up?

Anthony's reaction had been the opposite of hers. He'd been pleased and had started talking about how they would get married and buy a house together. Natalie had needed to yell at him to shut him up.

"I told you I never wanted kids!" she'd screamed.

He'd frowned. "I figured you'd change your mind and… Wait a second. Are you saying you aren't going to keep it?"

He'd proceeded to make her feel broken for not wanting a child.

She'd thought she was tough, thought she was good at taking shit, but he'd managed to crack through her defenses before she dumped his sorry ass. He'd made her feel unlovable.

Natalie was glad Sharon's experience was different.

She sighed.

Connor glanced at her. "You okay?"

"I'm fine." She didn't tell him what she'd been thinking about. She'd never told him why she'd broken up with Anthony.

He pulled up to her childhood home on Maple Grove Lane, and she pushed thoughts of babies and pregnancy and Connor's ex-wife out of her mind.

Time for brunch with her family. Hopefully, it wouldn't be too awkward.

Ha. Like there was any chance of this going well.

Natalie thanked her father when he handed her a plate with a slice of quiche. Then she helped herself to salad and bread, which she slathered with lots of butter and raspberry jam, and poured herself yet another cup of coffee. She looked around the table before stabbing her salad with her fork.

Someone was missing. Rebecca hadn't said anything yet, and neither had Seth, but Natalie figured it was time. She was about to open her mouth when Connor placed his hand on her thigh, and it felt so good that she momentarily forgot what she was going to say.

Right. She remembered now.

"Where's Mom?" she asked her father.

Dad shrugged and started eating his quiche.

Silence. Well, this was awkward.

Naturally, Simon was the one to fill it. He turned to Elliot and Rebecca. "Since you're not taking a honeymoon right away, are you two going back to work tomorrow?"

Elliot nodded, then looked at Rebecca. She squeezed his hand.

"I quit my job," she said.

"When did this happen?" Dad asked.

"Earlier this month. My last day was two Fridays ago."

"You found something better? When do you start?"

"Actually, I won't be working now that we're married." Rebecca gave Elliot a small smile.

Natalie couldn't believe this. It wasn't the 1950s. There was no reason to quit your job when you got married. She opened her mouth, then snapped it shut—her sister's wedding weekend brunch probably wasn't the time to question her life choices.

"I was unhappy with my job," Rebecca said, "and Elliot makes good money. We'll both be happier this way. I'll do most of the cleaning and cooking while he's at work, so we'll be able to relax when he gets home. It'll be nice. Plus, we'll start trying for a baby right away, and I want to be a stay-at-home mom for the first few years, until the kids start kindergarten."

Natalie stared at her younger sister, who'd won math and physics awards at the end of high school, who'd finished in the top ten percent of her class at university. And now Rebecca was quitting her job in engineering to cook and clean and make babies?

This wasn't what she wanted for her sister. This wasn't the way it was supposed to be.

"But your degree," Natalie said, unable to keep her mouth shut any longer. "You spent four years getting it, and now you're just going to give up?"

The smile slid off Rebecca's face. She put down her fork. "I spent four years studying something I hated, followed by three years of a job I hated. I've finally had enough. I'm not saying I'll never work again. I hope to, once the kids are in school, but I don't want to be an electrical engineer."

Natalie was confused. "You're so good at it."

"That doesn't change the fact that it made me miserable."

"Why don't you look for a new job? Surely with a degree and a few years of experience, you could find something else in the field in Toronto."

"You don't get it," Rebecca said, frustration in her voice. "It's not just that I didn't like the particular job I had. I didn't like the field at all, and I'm lucky I don't have to do it now. I have the chance to try something different, and I'm going to take it. Are you unhappy with my decision to have a family?"

"No."

Natalie thought being an aunt would be fun, and Rebecca would make a good mother. If her sister wanted kids, then Natalie wanted her to have them. However, Rebecca did seem a little young; most of the women Natalie knew had waited until they were over twenty-five. And after seeing what her mother had gone through when she was pregnant and then when Rebecca was a baby, Natalie was a bit worried. Having a child was tough.

But Rebecca quitting her job…

"What sort of work might you want to do later on?" Connor asked before reaching for the salad bowl.

"I don't know. I still have to figure it out."

"Then figure it out while you have an engineering job," Natalie snapped. "You'll still be able to take maternity leave and stay home with your child for a year, but then you can go back to work."

"I'm not going back to that job or anything like it. Why can't you understand that?"

"What if something happens? What if you and Elliot get divorced? You need to be able to support yourself. It'll be much harder if you take yourself out of the workforce for several years. Better to keep your job for now and put your child in daycare."

Rebecca shoved herself to her feet. "I got married two days ago, and you're already talking about me getting divorced? What's wrong with you? You think that just because you're not happily married, no one else is allowed to be, either?"

Natalie would likely never be happily married, it was true, and that stung.

"I thought Mom and Dad were happy," she shot back, "and look what happened there. You need to be prepared for the worst. What if Elliot dies, and you have three children to support?" She knew she was being an ass, but she couldn't seem to help it.

"Again, what's wrong with you? I know you think climate change is going to kill us all, but that doesn't mean the rest of us have to be doom and gloom all the time. There's something called optimism. Maybe you should look it up in the dictionary."

"Girls," Dad said. "Can we please eat our brunch in peace? Rebecca, Natalie only has your best interests at heart, even if she has a rather twisted way of expressing it. No need to argue."

God, Natalie felt like a child again. Except she and Rebecca had never argued like this when they were kids. Natalie had argued with Seth, but Rebecca, being so much younger than them, was different.

"I think you're jealous that I got married first," Rebecca said.

"I'm not jealous of someone who wants to be a housewife. You could do so much better."

"If this were a storybook, you'd be the miserable old spinster."

"But it *isn't* a storybook. It's real life."

"I bet you and Connor really are just friends after all."

"Natalie." Connor stood up and took her by the arm. "Let's go outside for some fresh air, okay?"

She didn't want to leave. She wanted Rebecca to change her goddamn mind.

"Please," he whispered. "I think you need a break. Just five minutes." His hand was warm on hers.

Fuck it. She would go with him.

The doorbell rang just before they reached the front door. She pulled it open.

"Hi, Natalie," Mom said.

"Why did you ring the doorbell? It's your house. Oh, wait…"

Dad came to the door. "Why are you so late? And why is Louisa here?"

"Hello, Howard," Louisa said. "Glad to see me?"

"You ruined my daughter's wedding. Of course I'm *delighted* to see you. At least you seem sober today."

"Why are you complaining about Rebecca's wedding?" Mom snapped. "You didn't even *want* her."

There was a very tense silence. Her parents stared at each other.

Both of them had always doted on Rebecca, except at the very beginning. Was this a reference to those early days? They never talked about that. But Natalie had too much on her mind right now to ponder it further.

"Alright, alright," Louisa said, heading toward the dining room. "Let's have some fun! Where's the wine?"

As Mom walked inside, Connor led Natalie outside. They sat on the steps.

"Dear God," she muttered. "I have a headache."

He opened his mouth, but she didn't let him speak.

"Don't you dare say anything. I don't need you telling me I'm wrong about Rebecca. I can't handle that right now."

"I wasn't going to say that. I'm here for you, Natalie." He put his arm around her and pulled her closer to his big body.

They sat in silence for several minutes, and the anger slowly seeped out of her veins. She still couldn't say she was happy, though. This wasn't the life she wanted for Rebecca. Married to a man she'd known less than a year, ready to pop out babies right away, and planning to stay home to take care of them and cook and clean.

No. Her little sister was smart and talented. She was destined for better things than this. Why couldn't Rebecca see that? Why didn't she believe in herself?

Where had Natalie gone wrong?

She had a strange relationship with Rebecca. It wasn't what

she thought of as a normal sisterly relationship—the age difference between them was too great. Natalie felt like she was somewhere between a sister and a parent.

But even though she had lots more to say on the subject, she would go back in there and apologize to Rebecca for questioning her life decisions. Her whole family was here under one roof, and that wasn't a frequent occurrence. It would be even less frequent in the future when—

Oh, dear God. Was that Uncle Dennis's car pulling up in front of the house?

Uncle Dennis stepped out of the driver's side, then helped his mother out of the car.

"Fuck, fuck, fuck," Natalie muttered, because she was just so eloquent.

"Were they supposed to come?" Connor asked.

"No. I assume Aunt Louisa invited them. I'm not in the mood to deal with my racist, homophobic relatives."

"Want me to get rid of them?"

"Please."

He walked down the driveway and halted before Uncle Dennis. She couldn't hear the conversation, but a minute later, her unwanted uncle and grandmother drove away.

That was surprisingly fast.

"What did you say to him?" she asked as Connor walked back to the house.

"I simply told them that you didn't want to deal with your racist and homophobic relatives right now."

"You did not."

"Not exactly, but I have my ways. I can be very persuasive." He winked at her.

She felt a strange flutter in her chest and smiled back at him.

She was grateful to him for putting out that fire for her; she was used to having to do everything herself. He'd been so attentive this weekend. A comforting, solid presence when everything was whirling around her.

They returned to the dining room, where Simon was chatting about a recent trip to Prague and doing his best to ignore the tension in the room.

Dad interrupted. "I thought I heard a car pull up."

"Dennis and Grandma," Natalie said. "Don't worry, they're gone now."

She glanced at Rebecca and wondered if her sister was going to say that Natalie should have invited them in. But Rebecca was silent.

Natalie had something she wanted to get off her chest, though. Although she'd planned to try to make peace with her sister, she couldn't seem to hold back now.

"I can't believe you invited them to the wedding," she said. "You know what they're like. They're awful."

"But they're family," Rebecca protested.

"Family doesn't trump everything. You don't have to think of those assholes as family. You have enough relatives who aren't bigots. Focus on those ones."

"Like the sister who thinks I'm screwing up my life by wanting to be a stay-at-home mom?"

I just want you to have it all, and that includes a career, as well as a husband and children. To be honest, Natalie was full of hope when it came to Rebecca. Her outburst earlier? She might have been talking about worst-case scenarios, but it really was born out of love and hope for her sister, even though she didn't think it was reasonable to have the same hope for herself. Natalie wished she could have it all, too—except for the babies, of course—but she didn't see how it was possible.

However, it should be possible for her sister.

"I'm only thinking of you," she said. "Grandma and Dennis, on the other hand, don't give a shit about you as a person."

"I think you're wrong about that."

"Maybe I am. Maybe they care a little, but that shouldn't matter to you when they're such horrible people. Do you think it was fair to expect Seth and Simon to be around them for a whole day, knowing they might make nasty comments at any moment? Grandma and Dennis need to learn that we won't put up with their shit."

Rebecca turned to Mom. "Do you agree I shouldn't have invited my own grandmother to my wedding? She's in her nineties—she's not going to change."

"Don't use her age as an excuse," Natalie snapped. "She didn't go to Mom and Dad's wedding, and she was hardly an elderly woman forty years ago. She's had ample opportunity to change, and she hasn't."

Nobody said anything.

Dad finally broke the silence. "Who wants dessert?"

The rest of brunch was an uncomfortable affair with stilted conversation. Mom and Dad made occasional digs at each other. Natalie refrained from speaking too much, afraid she would lash out at Rebecca. Rebecca was cheerful, but it seemed awfully fake, and Louisa acted like she was drinking, even though there was no alcohol.

At one o'clock, Natalie figured they'd better get going. It was a long drive back, and she and Connor had to work tomorrow.

She hugged her sister goodbye and said, "Congratulations on your wedding." Anything more and they might get into an argument. She couldn't bear another argument with Rebecca, but she was firm in her opinions. Her little sister should not have invited Dennis and Grandma to her wedding, and being a stay-at-home mother was not the right profession for her. So they gave each other a hesitant hug.

"I don't know when we'll be back next," Simon said, throwing his arms around Natalie. "Keep me posted on what's happening with Connor, okay?"

"We're just friends," she mumbled, and those words pierced her bruised heart.

Once all the goodbyes had been exchanged, they headed out to the car.

"Do you want to drive?" Connor asked.

She shook her head. "Not now. I've still got a bit of a headache."

When he pulled away from the curb, she closed her eyes but didn't sleep. Instead, she remembered the day her sister had come home from the hospital, scrunched up and crying but beautiful all the same.

[16]

THEY'D BEEN in the car for over two hours. Connor had driven the whole time and Natalie hadn't said a word. He figured she would talk when she wanted to.

Despite the awkward brunch, he wanted to be a part of Natalie's family, and he wanted to be there for her whenever she went home. He wanted everything that came with a serious relationship. After years of not being interested in such a life, it surprised him, but it was the truth.

"'I Loved Her First,'" Natalie said, and he was momentarily startled by her voice after hours of silence. "Do you know that song?"

"It's often played for father-daughter dances at weddings, isn't it?"

She nodded. "The first time I heard it, which was at a wedding, I nearly cried. Can you imagine? Me, almost crying at a wedding."

"I can imagine it," he said.

She shrugged. "Anyway, when I heard that song for the first time, I thought of me and Rebecca, even though it's a father talking about his daughter. Because that's how I feel about her.

Until she was about six months old, I was the one who would snuggle her and sing her songs and tell her I loved her. Just me. No one else. My mother didn't bond with her right away. I'm pretty sure she had postpartum depression." She paused. "Did you know I named my sister?"

"You did?"

"Well, I took a list of three names to my mother, and she picked her favorite."

"I've heard of parents asking an older sibling to name the new baby before. It doesn't usually work out well."

"There are some fucking awful names out there. Why do people do that to their kids?"

He liked when Natalie swore. He didn't know why, but it made him smile. Had it always been like that, or had it just started this weekend?

"My father," she continued, "didn't have much to do with Rebecca at the beginning, for whatever reason. Mom's cryptic comment about Dad not even wanting Rebecca—that was interesting. Was this what she was talking about? I don't know the story. All of a sudden, they're getting divorced, and I feel like I don't know my parents. I thought their love had survived so much, and it would continue to survive." She laughed without humor. "Listen to the lame words coming out of my mouth."

"Sometimes lame words are necessary."

Actually, there were some rather lame words he wanted to say to Natalie, but he wasn't sure he could ever get them out. He'd never been good at this stuff. Sharon had more or less taken the lead in their relationship, and it had been easier that way.

With Natalie, he knew he'd have to be the one to bring it up, and he wasn't sure he'd be successful, especially given what he felt obligated to reveal from the beginning.

"By Rebecca's first birthday," she said, "Mom and Dad seemed like themselves again, and they were loving parents to Rebecca."

"What about to you?" he asked.

"I was hitting that awkward pre-teen phase. I didn't really want my parents around."

"But looking back, what were they like with you then?"

"I don't know. All I remember is me and Rebecca together."

"You used to keep a picture of the two of you in your notebook, back in university."

"I did," she said. "It was hard for me to be apart from her, and I used to go home every two weeks. I know, it was lame."

"Why are you calling everything you say and feel lame?"

"Because it doesn't fit my image as a cranky old spinster."

"Rebecca doesn't really think that," he said. "When people get upset, they say things they don't mean."

"I know, I know. But I do think that's the way most people see me. The cranky, but otherwise emotionless, woman in her mid-thirties who's too dedicated to her career of predicting the end of the world to have time to find a man."

"I don't see you that way. As I showed you this weekend, I think you're very desirable."

The words hung in the air, and they were silent for a few minutes. They'd hit some heavy traffic on the 401 as they approached Toronto. No surprise; traffic around Toronto was always terrible. He hated driving near the city.

"Rebecca is more than a sister to me," Natalie said. "In some ways, I feel like her parent, too. Parents usually have certain expectations of their kids, and I always thought Rebecca would have a successful career in science or engineering." She sighed. "I know, I'm imposing my hopes on her. I'm judging her, the way people judge me for being single and childless at thirty-six. It's not fair, but I can't help it. Rebecca being a housewife, then a stay-at-home mom! I can't handle it."

"She was miserable at her job and didn't want to be an engineer."

"I know I should support her no matter what, but I can't wrap my mind around it."

"There's nothing wrong with being a stay-at-home mom."

"I can't imagine doing that."

"Not everyone is like you."

"Thank God for that," she muttered. "The world would be in serious trouble if that were true. Actually, the world is already in serious trouble. Flooding and heat waves—it's a mess."

They came to a stop. He hoped they wouldn't waste too much time getting through Toronto, though he couldn't say he minded spending more time with Natalie. But they were still a long way from Ottawa, and he'd prefer if their time together didn't involve a traffic jam.

He had to admit that the way Natalie cared for her sister—both when she was younger, and now—made his heart squeeze, but it also caused him sorrow. It was easy to imagine her as a mom.

And he couldn't give that to her.

"I also can't wrap my mind around the idea of Rebecca being a mother," Natalie said. "I mean, I think she'd be a good mother, but I can remember changing her diapers—it's hard to imagine her changing her own baby's diapers. Where has the time gone? How is my baby sister old enough to have a baby of her own? It freaks me out. Plus, I'm terrified she'll have postpartum depression like Mom. I know there are treatments, but nothing works a hundred percent of the time, does it?"

"There's lots that can be done, though." He paused. "Where was your extended family when Rebecca was born? Why didn't they help?"

"My father's family was in Toronto, and we didn't see them a lot. They still hadn't gotten over my parents' marriage. Uncle Carey was living in Alberta at the time, and Aunt Louisa was going through her second divorce, plus she had her own children to look after. Sometimes she came by and went for walks with Mom, leaving Rebecca with me. Grandma, Grandpa, and Uncle Dennis were useless. Grandma did stop by on occasion, but those were short, tense visits. Grandma seemed to like Rebecca the best of the three of us, and not just because she was the baby. I'm pretty sure it's also because she looks whiter than Seth and I do."

"That's disgusting."

"It is." Natalie paused. "I think we tried to protect Rebecca from our family, even when she was an adult, and we were mostly successful. That's probably why she was okay with inviting them to the wedding. She doesn't know how bad it is, and she's willing to tolerate more than I am, just because people are family. The things we do for family." She shook her head and sighed. "I'll have to call Rebecca in a few days. Maybe I'll go see her in a couple weeks. God, I hate that it's like this between us."

They were quiet again for a little while. As they were passing Bowmanville, Connor glanced over and noticed that Natalie's eyes were pink and she was silently crying.

"Darling." He wanted to put his arm around her and hold her, but he was driving.

He was about to tell her not to cry, then stopped himself. He didn't want her to feel like she wasn't allowed to cry. If she needed to cry, she could.

"This is embarrassing," she said.

"It's fine." He touched her leg. "I understand."

"You know what's really embarrassing? I cried during the last movie I watched."

"Which movie was that?"

"*Moneyball.*"

He smiled. "Okay, that's kind of embarrassing."

"Do you ever cry during movies?"

"I cried during *Eternal Sunshine of the Spotless Mind.*"

"Ooh. That's a good one. Makes much more sense than crying during *Moneyball.*"

"I also cried during *The Notebook,*" he admitted, "and I didn't even like the movie."

She chuckled at that, and he was glad he'd made her laugh.

He pulled off at the next service center and led her to a picnic table at the edge of the parking lot.

"It's okay," he said, wrapping his arms around her.

"I know. But sometimes it's hard to *really* know that. Does that make any sense?"

"It does."

"It's so complicated with Rebecca. And dammit, I wanted her to have the perfect wedding. But Aunt Louisa dropped that bombshell about our parents' divorce, and then today I had a fight with Rebecca at brunch. Things never work out the way they're supposed to."

He thought of Sharon. "No, they don't."

He nuzzled the side of Natalie's face, and she turned back and kissed him, a tentative kiss that he deepened. He didn't want this to end.

"Let's stop in Kingston for dinner," he said. "Unless you're still full from those Cheetos."

"No, dinner would be good. I didn't eat much at brunch."

Maybe at dinner he would admit his feelings for her. Then he'd tell her about how he saw his future. It wasn't the kind of conversation you could put off when you were thirty-six, and he owed her the truth, plus he wanted to know before he was in too deep.

But maybe he already was.

Unfortunately, he didn't see that conversation going well.

"You've been to this place before, I assume?" Natalie asked as they waited for a table at a wood oven pizzeria. When they'd gotten off the highway, she'd wondered how he knew where to go, then remembered he'd spent four years in Kingston when he'd gone to Queen's for med school.

"A bunch of times," he said.

She hesitated. "You went here with Sharon?"

"I did." He linked his hand with hers, as if in apology.

They were led to a table at the back. Natalie ordered a pizza with prosciutto, brie, and pear. Connor ordered one with mushrooms, sausage, tomato sauce, and other things. They also got a small salad to split, but when it arrived, it was practically spilling over the sides of a large plate.

She didn't know how to feel right now. She was full of so many complicated feelings, and it was just too much to sort out at the moment.

There was her fight with Rebecca and her parents' divorce… but it was Connor who was occupying most of her thoughts now. He'd been great this weekend—he'd always been great, but she'd never fully appreciated what he did for her until this weekend. He accepted her the way she was and anchored her when she needed it, and despite everything that had happened, she'd had a lot of fun with him this weekend.

He felt like more than a friend now. He'd made her feel *cherished*, for God's sake.

She really was abrasive and pessimistic, as Anthony had said; her argument with her sister had made that much clear. But somehow, that didn't put Connor off. She felt like he actually liked that part of her; she felt like she might be lovable after all.

Natalie had thought they could just have a weekend of fun, a weekend of sex, and now…

"So," she said, "back to work tomorrow, eh? It'll be a bit of a relief to get back to my job, even though I have to read over my master's student's thesis. There's something comforting in having a routine. My five cups of coffee in the morning—"

"*Five?*"

"I'm exaggerating a little. Most days I have three cups in the morning. Sometimes I do have five, but that's rare."

He didn't say anything, just regarded her over the top of his water glass, and as she looked into his brown eyes, the air seemed to whoosh out of her.

Oh, she was fucked.

So fucked.

She'd assumed she would get over Connor, more or less, when she returned to her regularly-scheduled life in Ottawa, but now she knew it wouldn't go away easily. And she couldn't have him, not for more than a weekend. Perhaps he did care for her as more than a friend, but she had a terrible track record with relationships. She couldn't bear to put Connor through what was almost certainly a doomed relationship. Besides, he likely wanted kids—she couldn't let herself forget that.

When they parted ways, it would hurt more than usual, because he was *Connor*, and she'd fallen hard for him.

The pizza arrived, and she inelegantly stuffed a piece in her mouth. It was delicious, but she couldn't fully appreciate it right now.

It was ten o'clock when they arrived back in Ottawa. Connor grabbed their suitcases and followed Natalie into her building.

As soon as they reached her condo, they were kissing. He didn't know who'd started it, but they were on each other as soon as the door closed behind them. He held her close and walked backward into the bedroom, his lips never leaving hers. Their clothes disappeared quickly, and he laid her down on the bed and began kissing her everywhere he could reach—he wanted as much of her as he could have.

Soon, he was above her and inside her. She cried out beneath him, and it was everything.

Afterward, she fell asleep with her head tucked against his chest. He could extricate himself from this position and quietly leave, but he didn't want to. He wanted to stay the night.

Since he would have to get up early to go home for some clean clothes before heading to work, he grabbed his phone out of his pocket and set the alarm. Then he ran his hand up and down Natalie's back. Her nearly-black hair was making an oddly-shaped halo around her head.

He was afraid that if he asked her, she would say no.

He was even more afraid that she would say yes…and then it would change to a no once she heard the rest of what he needed to say. She was thirty-six, like he was; she didn't have all the time in the world to waste on a man like him if she wanted a family.

Once upon a time, he'd thought that was in store for him, too. He'd gotten married when he was twenty-six, and when Sharon was halfway through residency, they'd started trying for a baby.

But with each month that passed without success, he'd felt relieved.

Finally, after ten months, Sharon had been a few days late.

He'd been terrified.

Then she'd gotten her period, and she'd been crushed. He'd tried to comfort her, even as he felt profound relief, but it seemed there was nothing he could say to console her.

After a year, they'd gotten checked out.

Sharon was fine, but Connor had a low sperm count.

She'd pushed onward, immediately talking about their options. He'd briefly considered doing it for her because she wanted it so badly, then realized he couldn't. He finally admitted to himself that he didn't want kids, and it wasn't something he could compromise on. Plus, things had been a little rocky with Sharon for several months. They weren't the sort of couple who argued; rather, they'd become distant from one another.

He'd shocked her by asking for a divorce, and once she'd accepted that it was the only way forward, he'd felt profoundly relieved once more. It wasn't the life he'd planned, but it was the one that was necessary, and he'd quickly gotten accustomed to being single again. He hadn't missed being married.

But now, he was thinking he might want that again, with someone else.

Connor looked down at Natalie, curled against him. Maybe he was wrong about her. She'd never mentioned wanting children, never talked about her ticking biological clock, despite being over thirty-five, and wasn't desperately looking for a man. Nor had she talked about going to a sperm bank and doing it alone, which was the kind of thing Natalie would do. She wouldn't be afraid of doing it by herself if she really wanted a kid. Well, maybe she would be, but she wouldn't let on that was how she was feeling.

Of course, when he and Natalie met up, they didn't usually talk about anything serious, and he'd never told her why he and Sharon had gotten divorced. Still, Natalie would have mentioned kids at some point if it was important to her, right?

It was silly of him to assume she wanted children because of how she'd looked after her sister. Connor liked kids, too, but he wanted them to go home to someone else at the end of the afternoon. He loved his niece and saw her regularly, but that didn't mean he wanted to be a dad.

He was thankful for his low sperm count, though he did find it a touch embarrassing. He knew he shouldn't, but he did, and he'd told very few people.

However, if it hadn't been for his low sperm count, he and Sharon probably would have conceived, and he'd have a son or daughter now. If he had a child, he would be the father figure he needed to be; he wouldn't have run from his responsibilities. But it was something he'd prefer not to do.

Would they still be married if they had a kid? What if he'd wanted it as much as she did?

No, he doubted they would have stayed together, not in the long run. He'd been slowly falling out of love with Sharon, which was why it had been easy to ask for the divorce when he realized he couldn't give her what she wanted. In retrospect, he and

Sharon had been too similar, aside from their opposite views on having children.

Natalie, on the other hand, was very different from him, but they seemed to fit together just right.

He smoothed his hand over her forehead. Perhaps it wasn't hopeless after all. He would ask her soon. He'd cook her a nice meal next weekend and make a big deal of it. Knowing Natalie, she'd probably roll her eyes, but she'd be secretly pleased.

So he hoped.

[17]

THE FOLLOWING SATURDAY AFTERNOON, Natalie was walking down Rideau Street when she saw a familiar face up ahead, coming toward her. Was that…?

Her heart pounded, and she considered turning down a side street to avoid him.

But she was a tough thirty-six-year-old woman. She did not need to hide from her ex, even if he just so happened to be pushing a stroller and walking beside another woman.

"Natalie!" He stopped when he was a few feet from her, in front of a shawarma and poutine restaurant. "How are you? It's so good to see you again."

The last time she'd seen Anthony, they'd screamed at each other, but that was four years ago. Now he was perfectly pleasant, though it turned Natalie's stomach to see him again, remembering how he'd made her feel broken. Unworthy.

Those feelings came rushing back with a vengeance.

"This is my wife, Carrie," he said. "And this is Hailey." He indicated the baby in the stroller. She was asleep, and she looked to be maybe two or three months old.

Natalie opened her mouth. She figured a "Congratulations" or an "I'm happy for you" might be in order. Maybe, "Oh my God, she's so cute!" However, the words stuck in her throat.

Instead, she thought of how Connor deserved what Anthony had. The pretty wife with blonde ringlets, the pink-cheeked baby.

And Natalie could not give that to him.

"What about you?" Anthony asked. "How have you been?"

"I've been great!" she said, though she was sure the faux cheer wasn't fooling anyone, not even Baby Hailey.

Natalie wasn't envious of Carrie. She had no interest in Anthony, though she couldn't help feeling a little pathetic in the face of familial bliss. Her ex had hit the standard milestones, and she hadn't. Though, of course, she didn't want all of them.

They exchanged a few more inane pleasantries—was it her imagination, or did Anthony seem rather smug?—before she headed to the liquor store to buy a bottle of wine to bring to Connor's tonight. Her hand shook as she pulled the bottle off the shelf.

She had to put an end to this. Had to set Connor free to pursue a woman who could give him all that he deserved.

He'd texted her a few days ago to invite her over for dinner, and she'd said yes, even though she didn't know exactly what was going on between them, even though it could never be anything lasting.

She considered calling to cancel their dinner plans, but she couldn't do it. She wanted him, and as she'd realized at their quasi-romantic pizza dinner on Monday, this wouldn't go away easily.

One more night. She'd allow herself one more night.

At six thirty, Natalie knocked on the door of Connor's town-home. She was holding a bottle of red wine, and underneath her jeans and blouse, she was wearing a bra and panties that actually matched.

Connor answered the door, and she grinned at the sight of him. She also felt a hitch in her breathing, and her heart stuttered in her chest. She reacted so strongly to him now. Two weeks ago, she hadn't felt any of this.

It was goddamn inconvenient, and it couldn't continue, but she pushed those thoughts aside. For now.

She handed him the bottle of wine.

"You didn't need to," he said as he put it down on the table.

And then he was kissing her, his fingers furiously unbuttoning her shirt. His mouth devoured hers as though he was parched with thirst.

Good. She didn't want to wait, either. She hadn't seen him in five days, and that felt like forever. She wanted to lose herself in his body, forget about her earlier trip down memory lane.

She pulled off his polo shirt and ran her hands over his large biceps. He worked out several times a week, she knew. When she raked her fingernails across his chest, he sucked in a breath. And when she unbuttoned her jeans and pushed them down, it seemed to render him speechless.

She'd always hated it when women in their mid-thirties said they were old, but she'd started to feel that way in the past year, started to feel like she wasn't as attractive as she'd once been. Yet with Connor, she felt like a wine that got better with age.

"I wore matching underwear," she said. "Just for you."

His gaze raked over her body and came to settle on her face.

"Just for you," she repeated, staring into his eyes.

She laughed as he hoisted her into his arms and carried her upstairs to the bedroom.

He set her down on the bed and lay on top of her, and oh, she loved the pressure of his body against hers, his skin against hers. But she was still wearing her bra, and her nipples strained toward him, begging for his touch.

He unfastened her bra and threw it on the ground; he knew exactly what she needed. He brushed his thumb over her peaked nipple before lowering his head and taking it in her mouth.

She couldn't help but moan.

She unzipped his pants and pushed them down along with his boxers. He stood up briefly to take them off, and then he was on top of her again, his erection pressing between her legs, so close to where she needed him but not quite there.

"Connor," she groaned.

His hand slid inside her panties—the last scrap of fabric between them—and somehow, before he touched her core, she had the presence of mind to register a noise from downstairs.

"I hate to say this." My God, did she ever hate to say this. "But do you have a pot on the stove? It sounds like something's bubbling over."

"Shit. The pasta water." He hurried downstairs in the nude to deal with the unfortunate interruption.

Natalie figured she might as well get naked, too. She'd just taken off her underwear when Connor ran back into the room and settled himself on top of her again.

"No more interruptions," he murmured. "I promise." He licked his finger and slid it between her legs, circling her clit a few times before pushing inside. "Is this better?"

"I think you know the answer to that." The last word changed to a moan as he began rubbing her nub with his thumb, and two of his fingers thrust in and out of her body. God, she loved it when he touched her. He bent his head and kissed between her legs, enhancing the pleasure, making it almost too much to bear.

She shattered in his arms.

"Natalie, Natalie," he said in wonder, as if she had just performed a miracle for him.

She reached for him, circling her hand around his shaft and moving up and down. His fingers were still inside her body, caressing her. Her lips trembled as she looked into his eyes.

He grabbed a condom from the bedside table and rolled it on. He entered her slowly, filling her up. Filling all of her. She couldn't imagine letting anyone but Connor inside her; he was all she wanted now.

He started moving within her, each thrust so blindingly intense. Dimly, at the back of her mind, she knew there were problems with the two of them being together, knew it wouldn't work out. But for now, they were here, and that was all that mattered.

She turned her body to the right, and he let her roll them over so she was on top, riding him. She sat up straight and cupped her breasts in her hands, stroking her nipples with her thumbs. She felt powerful here with him, and she wanted him to see everything she could be.

He moved his hips up to meet hers, and she bent down and kissed him, pressing her chest to his. It was so amazing, just feeling his skin against hers.

He flipped her over easily—he was much bigger than her, and so strong, and she loved it—and picked up his pace. The sex became frenzied, and she met each of his quick strokes until he cried out. She followed him a moment later.

Connor stayed inside her, just for a few seconds. His face was slick with sweat, which was rather sexy, and he was breathing heavily.

Natalie was in post-coital bliss. If only they could stay here forever.

But when he pulled out, something was very wrong.

She sat up. "What the hell happened to the condom?"

[18]

Natalie's heart sped up. She knew she shouldn't panic, but she couldn't help it.

"Shit," Connor said, looking at the broken condom.

She jumped up, ran to the washroom, and sat down on the toilet.

It's okay, she told herself. *You're going to be okay.*

But all she could think of was Anthony, who'd somehow managed to get her pregnant even though they'd had no problems with condoms breaking or leaking. None that she'd noticed, anyway. She remembered telling him about the positive pregnancy test. He'd been excited about the future, while she'd felt like the world was crashing down on her.

She shook her head. She needed to think sensibly about this. First, since there was the possibility of pregnancy, she needed to head to the pharmacy and get the morning-after pill. She wasn't looking forward to that part. The only time she'd taken the morning-after pill, she'd had nausea and stomach pain.

Okay. She exhaled. She would take the pill, and if she still got pregnant, that would be pretty damn unlucky.

But after what had just happened, she wasn't feeling particularly lucky.

There was a knock on the door.

"Natalie," Connor said, "can you please come out so we can talk?"

She must have been in the washroom for a while. She'd lost track of time.

"Just a moment." She felt tears pricking at the back of her eyes. She splashed water on her face before opening the door.

He pulled her against his body and hugged her before leading her back to the bedroom.

"I don't want to have this conversation in the nude," she said.

He nodded before putting on his boxers and pulling out a black T-shirt from his dresser—the polo shirt he'd been wearing earlier was downstairs. He threw her a Queen's University shirt.

"First of all," he said, as she was struggling to pull the enormous shirt over her head, "I've had one other sexual partner since the last time I was tested."

He sounded so calm. Like a doctor.

Well, that made sense.

"I always used condoms with her," he continued, "but, of course, there's still a chance. I will get tested immediately and let you know. And you?"

"Haven't been with anyone but you since I was tested a year ago, and all the tests were negative."

She finally got the T-shirt over her head. The sleeves went down to her elbows, and God help her, but she liked wearing this shirt, which smelled faintly of *him*. She pulled her knees up to her chest under the large shirt.

"Are you on any other kind of birth control?" he asked. "The pill, an IUD…"

She shook her head. She'd tried the pill before—a few different ones, in fact—but had experienced unpleasant side effects.

"I assume you'll want to take the morning-after pill," he said, "but before you go to the pharmacy, I want you to know—"

"*No*," she snapped, her argument with Anthony flashing through her mind. "There is no fucking way I'm having your baby. Don't tell me this is a sign from God or the universe or whatever the hell you believe in. I'm not doing it. I'm taking the morning-after pill, and if that doesn't work, I'm getting a goddamn abortion. I've done it before, and I don't want to do it again, but I will if I need to. There will be no baby and don't you dare call me selfish for not wanting to have my life upended like this."

The fire left her voice. She did feel a bit selfish, actually, continuing on with Connor tonight when she couldn't give him everything, when she knew she had to let him go.

He tilted his head to the side and regarded her for a moment. "I would never say that. I just wanted to tell you that I have a low sperm count, so the chance of you getting pregnant is very slim, even if you don't take the morning-after pill. But you can take it for your own peace of mind."

It took a minute for her brain to comprehend his words, and once she did, she almost laughed. The condom had broken, but she'd just so happened to be with a man who had a low sperm count. Yes, that was rather reassuring, though she would still go to the pharmacy.

"How do you know you have a low sperm count?" she asked.

"Sharon and I were trying to have a baby. After a year without success, we both got checked out and discovered that the problem was me."

He'd just confirmed what she'd already been sure of. He wanted a baby. The men she slept with always did. She'd known that, but now that he'd said it, she felt an ache in her chest.

"Tell me about the abortion." He sat behind her and wrapped his arms around her waist. "It sounds like it really upset you."

She relaxed, just a tiny bit, against him. "The abortion itself didn't upset me, but the circumstances around it did." Her voice was a touch shaky. "Do you remember Anthony? I think you met him a couple times."

"Is he the one who worked for the government?"

"It's Ottawa. A lot of people work for the government."

"Did he have a moustache?"

"He did have one for a while. It looked stupid on him." She paused. "We always used condoms, but somehow, I got pregnant. I knew what I was going to do, but I figured I'd tell him about it. I mean, he was my boyfriend, right? As soon as the word 'pregnant' came out of my mouth, he got all excited and talked about moving in together and how it was a 'sign.' God, it was awful." She wrapped her arms more tightly around her knees. "I told him to go fuck himself—"

"Of course you did," Connor murmured.

"And I told him I was getting an abortion, no matter what his feelings were on the matter. He was offended that anyone would ever think of aborting something that had been fertilized with his sperm. He said he was pro-choice, but it sounded like he'd harshly judge any woman he knew, not just his girlfriend, for making this particular choice. He told me he would propose if I kept it, and I—"

"Told him to go fuck himself again?"

"Yeah. Pretty much." She fiddled with the hem of her shirt. She was going to tell Connor the truth now; it seemed like the right time to do it. This, presumably, would be the end of whatever was between them.

Earlier she'd freaked out on him, remembering what had happened with Anthony, but she knew he wouldn't respond like her ex and call her names when he learned she never wanted to be a mother.

However, he'd just admitted to trying to have a baby with his ex. They were not compatible.

Although she'd known Connor for years, it felt like she'd just found him, and now she would lose him again. She'd put off telling him in part because she'd wanted to be able to fantasize that it would work out, but it was time to put an end to those silly fantasies.

It was time for the cold, hard truth. She'd planned to end this tonight anyway, even before the broken condom.

Interesting that she'd never told him before about not wanting kids; he was a good friend, after all. She'd told some of her friends, like Kara, but maybe it had seemed more awkward with a male friend.

"The thing is…" She didn't look at him; it was easier this way. "The thing is, I don't want to have a baby at all. Not just with Anthony, but with anyone. I don't want to get pregnant and give birth, nor do I want to adopt. I don't want to raise a kid. It's not that I don't think I'm capable of it—actually, I'm pretty sure I could do it, though I doubt I'd be an amazing mom. But I don't want to, and my mind isn't going to change the instant you put a baby in my hands, and I highly doubt I'll regret it when I'm older. I'm thirty-six. I know myself by now. Yes, it's partly because I don't want to bring a child into this overpopulated, fucked-up world with the scary rise in global temperatures, but that's only a small part of it. It's just not for me. And it's not because I'm selfish or don't like children—"

"Natalie."

She didn't blame him for interrupting. She'd been rambling, trying to refute everything that had ever been said to her. Putting off the moment when they would go back to just being friends, when they would no longer snuggle up together, partially clothed, on his bed.

He put his hands on her shoulders and turned her around to face him. To her surprise, he was smiling.

"Of course I don't think you're selfish," he said, "and I believe you when you say you won't change your mind. In fact, I don't want children, either."

She couldn't make sense of his words. It had been such a long week. She must be imagining this. "You don't?"

"I thought I did, but I was relieved when Sharon didn't get pregnant. When she suggested IVF and adoption, that's when I knew for sure it was something I never wanted. It was the beginning of the end of our marriage."

She stared at him, still unable to wrap her mind around this.

After Anthony, she'd been serious about dating for a year, determined to find someone like her. But inevitably, she'd been attracted to men who wanted to start a family and who assumed that, being a childless woman in her thirties, she must be desperate to do so, too. They seemed to think she was motherly, although what it was about her that screamed "mother," she wasn't sure.

And after she'd changed her online dating profile to say "child-free," she'd gotten nothing but dick pics and offensive messages using the word "exotic" or similar. Not that she hadn't gotten those before, but they quickly became the *only* things she received.

Oh, the joys of online dating.

She'd reluctantly accepted that she'd never have a real future with a man. She couldn't find a half-decent guy who wanted what she did and liked her as she was.

But now, a man was saying he wanted the same thing as her, a man she very much desired.

It was exactly what she wanted, and she couldn't comprehend it.

"Last weekend," Connor said, "I was thinking about us being together, but I assumed you wanted a family. Then I started thinking…maybe I shouldn't assume that. You'd never talked about it, after all. And I was right." He pulled her closer. "After I made you dinner tonight, I was going to ask if you wanted to see each other—not just as friends who sometimes end up in bed together. I was going to tell you about not wanting to have kids since, especially at our age, it's best to be upfront about that sort of thing. But things didn't work out as planned, so…" He took her hands and squeezed them. "Natalie Chin-Williams, will you go out with me? It's only been a week since I first kissed you, but we've known each other for nearly two decades. I know I want this to be something serious, and I mean it when I say I just want it to be the two of us, not the two of us plus a houseful of kids."

She pictured the two of them on their wedding day. It had only been a week since they'd become more than friends, but she knew she wanted that eventually. Oh, she wanted it. With him.

Perhaps it really was possible after all…

No, it wasn't.

It was too good to be true.

Fantasies did not become reality, not for her.

She thought of her parents. If they couldn't make it, how did she have a hope? She was cranky and bad-tempered and so very used to being alone. She would screw up any relationship. It was inevitable, and she couldn't bear to screw things up with Connor Douglas, didn't want to put him through that when he'd already gone through a divorce. He was too good for her; he deserved better.

Which was exactly what she'd thought this afternoon. The circumstances were a little different now that he'd revealed he didn't want a chubby-faced baby, but she still knew it was true.

"Darling," he said, sliding his hand under her chin and tipping her face up.

And, oh, that word undid her, but she wouldn't let herself break down, not now.

"I can't do this," she said.

He frowned. "You don't want to be together?"

"Sex doesn't mean a woman wants a relationship."

"I know. But it feels like something more to me, and I thought you felt the same way." He paused. "You said you *can't* do this, but what you mean is that you don't *want* to do this?"

"Yes. That's right."

He looked at her skeptically, and he was right to be skeptical. She did want this, very much so. She just didn't see how they could possibly make it work, how *she* could possibly make it work. She was terrible at these things. She thought back to her fight last weekend with Rebecca, to her many ex-boyfriends… It was silly to think this would be any different, just because it was Connor and he didn't want children.

She needed to extricate herself from this situation right away.

"I should go," she said, starting to get up.

"Natalie, don't do this."

"I don't want you!" she shouted.

His face collapsed at her words, and it pained her withered, blackened heart to see him like that, but this was for the best. It was the only real option.

He climbed out of bed and tried to put his arms around her. "Tell me what's going on."

She pushed him away. "I'll get dressed, go to the pharmacy to buy the morning-after pill, and head home."

"I was planning to make you dinner."

"It was going to be romantic, and I don't want that."

"Please," he said quietly. "I love you."

She froze.

He didn't just like her for who she was—he loved her.

She didn't know what to do with that, couldn't fully comprehend it. Last weekend, he'd made her hopeful, made her feel like maybe she wasn't unlovable…and she'd considered herself foolish for believing that.

For a moment, she wondered if perhaps she hadn't been foolish after all, but then the truth came rushing back. Perhaps they could have a few good months together, but she couldn't imagine it would be more than that, not for a cantankerous woman like her with a long history of failed relationships. She would mess it up. He would fall out of love with her.

It would be less painful to put an end to this now. Why try something that she knew was doomed? That would truly be selfish.

She turned away from him without returning his words, without accepting them.

Five minutes later, she was walking to the bus stop.

When she paid for the pill at the pharmacy, her lip quivered, and she thought she might cry. But Natalie Chin-Williams did not cry, except during *Moneyball* and after uncomfortable brunches with her family, and she forced the tears back.

Connor would have come to the pharmacy if she'd let him. He would have looked after her if she got nauseous from the pill. He would have held her in his arms all night. But she wouldn't let him do any of that.

He needed better than her. He deserved better. And it would never last between them anyway.

She sent him a text. *Please get tested and send me the results.*

ARIANA DREW a purple squiggle on a piece of paper. She added a large, somewhat circular head with two eyes and a smiling mouth. "It's a snake!"

"I can see that," Connor said. His niece was sitting at her kid-sized table, and he was on the floor beside her.

"Now I'm going to make a map of the world." Ariana got out a fresh piece of paper. In the corner, she drew a house and a rectangle with her purple crayon. "This is our house, and that's daycare. Can you label them for me, please?"

He grabbed a pen and did as asked. After all, she'd used the magic word.

She drew a few red blobs, then shifted the paper toward him again. "Daddy's work, Ottawa, and Montreal."

He didn't point out that the house, daycare, and her father's work were actually within Ottawa.

"Uncle Connor." She scrunched up her face. "Something's wrong with you today."

"Nothing's wrong," he said. "I'm happy to see you, Ariana."

Which was true, but his mind kept wandering back to Natalie, hurrying down the sidewalk last night. Away from him. She would return to her condo and take the morning-after pill, and she would do it all alone. He knew she could handle whatever life threw at her, but he didn't want her to be alone.

He was still confused by the whole thing. It had been a jumble of emotions: first the condom had broken and she'd freaked out, then he'd realized that neither of them wanted children and there was nothing standing in the way of them being together. He'd been elated…and then she'd told him she didn't want anything more with him, which he still didn't believe. He'd known Natalie for a long time, and he could read her. It was more complicated than she let on, but she wouldn't open up to him.

Ariana pointed to a green blob. "This is England." Next, she drew a red stick. "This is the North Pole, where Santa Claus lives. I wish Santa Claus came on my birthday, but he only comes at Christmas."

He tried to push thoughts of Natalie aside and focus on his niece's drawing.

Except he couldn't stop thinking about her. They could look after Ariana together, and then they could go home and split a bottle of wine and stay up late watching a movie because they wouldn't have children of their own.

Ariana poked his arm. "Please label this for me. This is India, and this is France."

Interestingly, India and France were right next to each other.

"And this is Germany."

Germany was on the opposite side of the page from France.

She drew a large blue circle. "Here is the ocean, and here is Niagara Falls."

By the time Ariana got tired of her map fifteen minutes later, he'd labeled over twenty places for her, including New York City —which was separate from the United States—Vancouver, Toronto, and China, as well as the playground down the street. He wasn't in a great mood, but he could still smile at his four-year-old niece's view of the world.

When Mallory returned, they were playing zookeeper. Connor was a camel. When Ariana saw her mother, she hurried over to her table and proudly held up her map. "Look what I made, Mommy! Uncle Connor labeled it for me, but soon I'll be big enough to write the words myself." Her mouth opened in a wide circle. "Oh no! I forgot to draw Canada."

A few minutes later, Connor walked to the door with Mallory.

"How was your long weekend?" she asked. "Whatever you did, I bet it was more fun than trying to convince a four-year-old to put away her toys."

"I was at a wedding out of town," he said, purposely vague.

"Are you sure you're still willing to babysit Ariana next weekend?"

"I am." The plan had been for Natalie to help him, but he didn't know if she would show up. He wouldn't force her to be there. "You can relax and enjoy your weekend at the spa. Try not to call me every hour to see if Ariana has destroyed my house."

"I'll do my best."

That night, he ordered Thai food and wished Natalie was there to share it with him. Then he watched *Moneyball*. By some miracle, he managed not to cry during a movie about sports statistics, though there were moments when it was almost painful to breathe because she wasn't snuggled up against him.

Natalie did not have a great week. She went to work like usual, drank a lot of coffee, and finished reading her student's thesis, but she felt hollow inside. Whatever she did, she imagined doing it with Connor instead, and that always sounded so much better.

It's not possible.

She told herself that again and again.

She texted Rebecca and asked if she could visit her that weekend. Rebecca said sure, she could come, and Mom would also be in Toronto, staying with Bernard. Natalie still couldn't wrap her head around the idea of her mother being with someone other than her father. It seemed all wrong.

Everything felt wrong these days. There was Connor and Rebecca and her parents...

And Natalie was all by herself, which was normal for her, but it didn't feel right anymore.

She was on the train from Ottawa to Toronto now, a trip she'd made many times before. It was Friday afternoon, and she'd left the university earlier than usual. She had some journal articles to read, but she couldn't concentrate.

A few rows in front of her was a father with his two kids. It seemed like she saw kids every damn time she opened her eyes, and they always reminded her of her conversation with Connor.

How annoying.

She sighed and looked out the window. They were approaching Kingston, which, unfortunately, also reminded her of Connor.

Dammit. They'd driven across the province together, and now everywhere made her think of him. It had been an awful idea to take him to Rebecca's wedding.

Except it had been so nice to have him there, and it was hard to regret what had happened between them when it had felt so wonderful.

But for now, she needed to focus on what she would say to Rebecca. She needed to apologize and make things right again; she couldn't bear to have a strained relationship with her sister. There were already so many problems in the world, and she didn't need this on top of everything else.

When Natalie arrived at Rebecca and Elliot's apartment, they all acted like nothing had happened. Until Elliot left for the evening to visit his mother, leaving Natalie alone with Rebecca.

Her sister made some jasmine tea, and the two of them sat at the dining room table in silence, waiting for the tea to steep. Rebecca was no longer her cheery self.

Natalie wasn't good at these sorts of conversations, but she would do a lot of things she wouldn't normally do if they were for Rebecca.

"I wish your wedding had been…perfect," she said hesitantly.

Rebecca poured two cups of tea. "We don't need to talk about the wedding. Yes, it wasn't what I'd hoped for, but I'm married to Elliot, and that's what matters the most. You think I'm a little young, and I won't bring up Mom and Dad now, but Seth was even younger than me, and he and Simon are still married. But why do you have so many strong opinions on what I should do with my life? Why am I such a disappointment to you?"

Natalie's heart ached at those words. She hated that Rebecca saw it this way, but she understood. "You're not a disappointment to me. I promise."

"You're unhappy I quit my job."

"It just wasn't what I'd expected."

"You want me to be a brilliant electrical engineer. A shining example in a field with few women. From the time I was young, you talked about all the things I could do because of my aptitude for math and science. You had big dreams for me."

Natalie twisted her hands together. "You were always *mine*, Rebecca. I know you don't remember a time before we all doted on you, but when you were a baby, I think Mom had postpartum depression, and Dad wasn't around much, for whatever reason. I'm sure they loved you; they just couldn't show it. But I could. I spent lots of time looking after you. The stories and songs…I was the one who did all that."

"You were only eleven when I was born."

"I was young, but I did a lot. That was okay, because I'd always wanted a sister and loved you very much." Natalie's voice trembled. "Anyway, I guess…I felt a bit like a parent to you, with the sort of dreams and expectations for you that parents often have. When you were so amazing at math and science and computers, I couldn't help but think of all the things you could do with your talents."

"Except I hated those subjects in school."

"And I told you that's because you were bored and they were taught poorly."

"Which was true," Rebecca said, "but even in university, I wasn't interested. I kept waiting for that to change, and it never did."

"You could have switched your major."

"To what? I didn't know, and I didn't want to disappoint everyone. Not just you, but *everyone*. Society. I was a woman in engineering, and I was good at it. I felt like I would be disappointing my gender if I gave it up. I told myself it would be different once I started working, but it wasn't. Every day, I'd stare blankly at the wall in my office and think about hitting my head against it because I hated it all so much. When I said I was unhappy, I was understating it, and it felt like you wanted me to stay miserable."

"Of course not," Natalie said hurriedly. "I want you to be happy more than anything."

"That's not how you made me feel when we had brunch."

"I know. I'm so sorry about what I said. I was wrong."

She thought of all the times over the years that Rebecca had told her how much she hated her math homework, even though it was a breeze, or her electronics class, and Natalie had always reassured her that things would be different one day. She'd never considered the alternative—that Rebecca would never like those subjects. She'd assumed her little sister *had* to like them, since she had such an aptitude for them.

"It was Elliot," Rebecca said, "who made me see that I had

options. I didn't have to continue working in a field I hated. Since we want to have kids soon, I thought it would make sense to focus on that for a few years while I try to figure out everything else. I'm lucky he makes enough money that this is possible. But then you talked about him divorcing me. I'm not an idiot, Natalie. I know things don't always work out, but I wouldn't have married him if I didn't have faith that it would. Although after Aunt Louisa's interruption, I admit my faith was a little shaken."

"I was always proud of Mom and Dad for being able to do what they did in the seventies. I knew things weren't perfect, but I believed in them."

Rebecca squeezed Natalie's hand. "I'm sorry I called you a miserable old spinster. I didn't mean it, but sometimes, Nattie, I don't know quite what to think of you. What *do* you want?"

Natalie smiled at her sister's old nickname for her and had a sip of tea, delaying her answer. "I have what I want." Her voice wavered. She couldn't help it.

"You can be greedy and want more. Everyone is always making comments about you having kids and getting married, saying you're running out of time, but do you want those things? You never talk about them, and I don't know if it's too painful for you to talk about because it hasn't happened for you, or if you don't want it at all. Either way, you shouldn't have to put up with all those questions."

Natalie swallowed. "I don't want kids. I realized that when I was young. Mom's pregnancy with you was pretty rough, so that was part of it, and as much as I loved taking care of you, it also showed me that I didn't want to raise a kid of my own. Plus, the planet is overpopulated and going to shit. But I don't have a problem with *you* having kids, and I'd like to be an aunt. Part of the reason I freaked out on you, though, was because I was afraid your pregnancy would be like Mom's. I was also afraid you'd have awful postpartum depression, and I couldn't bear to think of it."

She must have looked like she was going to cry, because Rebecca reached across the table and patted Natalie's hand. Natalie was reminded of all the times she'd had to comfort a crying Rebecca, and the reversal of roles was…odd.

"I'll be fine," Rebecca said, "and if I need help, I'll get it. But first I need to get pregnant. That could take a while." She paused. "So, you don't want kids—"

"And that's totally fine. There's nothing wrong with it. I'm not selfish for feeling that way."

"I'm not judging you. You'll have more time to spend with my kids, and Seth and Simon's. Seth said they're going through the adoption process. I don't know if he told you, but it's not a secret."

"I knew they were going to, but I didn't know they'd started."

Rebecca sipped her tea. "Do you want to get married?"

Natalie shrugged. "It's not going to happen."

"That's not what I asked. Do you *want* to?"

Natalie nodded, unable to say the word.

"But you're bitter and have sworn off love because you've been hurt? Or you don't believe in love anymore?"

"It's stupid not to believe in love when there's so much evidence to the contrary."

She loved her sister and the rest of her family—the non-bigoted people, anyway. She'd experienced romantic love before and knew she'd come to love Connor if she wasn't careful.

But she was careful. She'd ended it.

Because she also knew that a year from now, Connor wouldn't be able to say "I love you" to her anymore. Yes, she believed in love, but she still didn't believe it could last for her. Though he'd made her hope, briefly, that it was possible.

"What about Connor?" Rebecca asked. "Honestly, I was so happy when I saw you two together that morning at the bed and breakfast. Something did happen, didn't it?"

"Yes." Natalie reached for the teapot and filled up their teacups.

"Does he want kids?"

"He doesn't, but I just don't think it's going to work out. And that's okay."

Rebecca hesitated. "You push people away sometimes, but when you were with him, you had a different dynamic. He was attentive, and you let yourself be taken care of for once, rather than the other way around. Did you push him away later?"

"That's between me and him," Natalie said, tensing.

God, she'd probably ruined their long friendship, too. No more hiking and cross-country skiing and drinking beer together. No more of his steady presence in her life.

The thought filled her with sorrow.

Rebecca reached for her hand again. "You'll find someone. I promise."

"Thanks, Mrs. Optimistic."

"And I will find something other than electrical engineering. I always envied you for knowing what kind of career you wanted."

"I changed my mind a bunch of times."

"But it was always something related to environmental science."

"True." Natalie looked down at their hands and a memory came to mind. "Remember all those times we played wedding together and I helped you marry Misty Gorilly and Fuzzy Wuzzy?"

"Of course. You made origami flowers for my bouquet—they were so pretty. And a crown when I wanted to marry a prince so I could become a princess. Fuzzy Wuzzy sure made an unconventional prince."

Natalie smiled. She'd forgotten those details. "Again, I apologize for what I said and for making our family brunch so miserable."

Rebecca nodded. "We're okay now. And you were right about Grandma and Uncle Dennis. I shouldn't have invited them."

"To be fair, we did shield you from what they were like, so maybe you didn't realize the extent of it. When Seth came out—I think you were ten—it was pretty awful."

"I might not have known then, but I figured it out later on. I just wanted so badly for us to be one big happy family and couldn't accept that some things aren't possible, no matter how much we want them."

Yes, Natalie knew that all too well.

"You're thinking about Connor, aren't you?" Rebecca asked. "That's different, and I think you should be optimistic about it." She paused. "You deserve it, Natalie. You know that, don't you?"

But the word "yes" refused to leave Natalie's lips.

[20]

Saturday morning, Natalie plodded up the steps to Bernard's small—but surely expensive—house in Forest Hill. She'd never been here before; she hadn't even known of the man's existence until two weeks ago.

Two weeks since Rebecca's wedding. God, so much had changed in that time. Hard to believe it had only been two weeks.

Her mother had asked if she wanted to meet Bernard, and Natalie had said she wasn't ready for that yet. Maybe the next time she came to Toronto. So Bernard had gone out golfing this morning, and her mother answered the door and showed her inside the cozy house.

Mom prepared the French press. She knew where everything was. How many times had she been here before?

"I want to ask you a question," Natalie said.

Mom sat down at the kitchen table. "I'm sure you have lots of questions."

Natalie hesitated. "You made a comment about how Dad hadn't wanted Rebecca. What did you mean?"

Based on the way her mother's eyebrows rose, Natalie

guessed she was surprised by the question. But of all that had happened, these were the words that haunted Natalie the most.

"I don't want Rebecca to know," Mom said, "but I'll tell you. I think it'll help you make sense of a number of things." She paused. "We had always planned to have two kids. Just two. The third pregnancy was unplanned, and your father wanted me to have an abortion. I'd always assumed that's what I'd do if I got pregnant again, but when I found out, I already loved her—I just knew she was going to be a girl—and I decided to keep her. I wouldn't do otherwise. Your father was pissed. He complained about all the expenses, and he didn't want to deal with diapers again. We fought throughout the entire pregnancy, which was probably part of the reason why I felt so ill."

It turned Natalie's stomach to think of her mother having an abortion, even though she had nothing against abortion and didn't regret her own. But the thought of her sister never existing...

"And then she was born," Mom said, "and when I looked at her, she didn't feel like *mine*. She did when I found out I was pregnant and she was just a tiny cluster of cells, yet when she was a real, screaming baby, I didn't care. Howard, who'd never wanted her anyway, didn't feel any differently. I bawled my eyes out when we drove home from the hospital, feeling like I'd made an awful mistake. I hadn't felt this way about you or Seth, and your dad hadn't been like this with you two, either. He didn't say anything in the car. It was all so...cold." She wiped her eyes before pouring two cups of coffee, her hand shaking on the French press. "But you were thrilled with her, and I was glad that at least she had that much. You carried her around and introduced her to all your stuffed animals."

"I remember," Natalie said. "I remember all of it. I knew something was wrong, and I wanted to give her the affection she needed."

"And I was the mother who couldn't bond with her own baby.

I felt so guilty. So overwhelmed by everything I had to do for her."

"Don't blame yourself. I'm sure many other women feel that way, even if they don't talk about it."

"I know I had postpartum depression. Eventually, your father forced me to see a doctor." Mom blew her nose. "It was several months before he started to feel affection for Rebecca, and I was annoyed that he did before me, when he was the one who'd wanted me to have an abortion."

Natalie still couldn't get over the idea of her sister never existing, but if she'd never had a sister, she wouldn't know what she was missing. There were so many directions her life could have taken, but in the end, you only got one shot at it all. It wasn't a *Choose Your Own Adventure* book in which you could read a bunch of different stories.

"Anyway," Mom said, forcing a smile, "within a year, everything was okay, more or less. But that was the beginning of the end of our marriage."

"Yet you stayed married for another twenty-five years. In fact, you're still legally married."

"We both felt so guilty about Rebecca, and we couldn't bear for her to have divorced parents."

"Having divorced parents isn't the end of the world."

"But it was Rebecca."

And really, that was enough of an answer. Rebecca, the baby of the family, was special; they all wanted everything to be perfect for her.

"You gave me hope," Mom said. "When I saw how much you loved spending time with her, it made me believe that one day, I would feel the same way. One day, everything would be okay. And, Natalie, I'm sorry I wasn't much of a mother to you then, either. Although you looked after Rebecca, you were still just a child."

Natalie nodded, then blurted out, "I had an abortion." For

some reason, she needed her mother to know this, even if Mom would never look at her the same way again. "If I hadn't terminated it, you would have a three-year-old grandchild."

Mom tilted her head and slowly nodded. "You don't owe me grandchildren. I haven't bugged you about that lately, have I?"

That was true. She hadn't, even if everyone else kept making comments about it.

"Do you feel guilty about the abortion?" Mom asked.

"When it was taken care of, I felt so relieved, and I think that's common. I don't regret it at all. I never want to have children."

Mom nodded again. "I know, honey."

"You do? You told me more than once that I'd change my mind when I was older. The first time, I was ten, and I was pissed you didn't take me seriously. I knew I was old enough to know my own mind."

Her mother chuckled. "I remember that. I think I was taken aback by the conviction in your voice at such a young age. But about ten years ago, someone—I can't remember who—made a comment about babies, and I could tell by the look on your face. You didn't want one, and you never would. I was a little disappointed, but I was glad you'd figured it out before actually having a child."

"Me, too."

"The last thing I want is for you to regret having a child. I felt like that for almost a year, and it was awful." Mom had a sip of coffee. "Come here."

Natalie stood up and went to her mother, and Mom embraced her. They were not an affectionate family, except with Rebecca, and it felt a little odd. But in a good way.

"You're okay," Mom said. "Your decisions are okay. I'm proud of you."

"Have you been reading too many self-help books?" Natalie joked, but somewhere deep inside, she felt her mother's words filling up an empty part of her.

"No. I just know you need to hear those words."

After leaving Bernard's, Natalie headed to her grandmother's house near Chinatown. Her feelings were a confusing mix of things she could not articulate, and she wished Connor was there to put an arm around her.

Dammit. If only…

You can have him, a voice inside of her whispered. *You can.*

She still didn't see how that was possible. How could someone like her make a relationship work, even if they agreed on not having kids?

But despite her melancholy mood, she couldn't help smiling when Ngin Ngin opened the door.

"Natalie! You're the last one here. Come in and meet my friend." Ngin Ngin put a frail hand on Natalie's back and ushered her inside.

Natalie entered the dining room, where Iris and Rebecca were standing around the table. An elderly white woman was perched on one of the chairs.

"Ngin Ngin, you should have let me get the door," Iris said.

"No. My house. I get the door. Everyone knows I walk slow. They can wait." Ngin Ngin turned to the elderly woman. "Rosetta, this is my oldest granddaughter, Natalie. Now you have met all granddaughters. Grandson is in Vancouver." She turned back to Natalie. "Rosetta is spring chicken!"

Natalie looked at her cousin and sister with raised eyebrows.

"Did I get that wrong?" Ngin Ngin asked. "It's a new phrase I learned yesterday."

"'Spring chicken' means a young person," Iris said.

Ngin Ngin nodded. "Exactly. Rosetta is spring chicken. Only eighty-one years old!"

Rosetta laughed. "Only you would say that."

"We met at the community center," Ngin Ngin said. "We go there to practice English. Rosetta is like me, except she comes from Italy. Spent life looking after husband and children, no time to learn proper English. So now we're old, we have time. Nobody comes to visit me."

"What?" Iris said. "I visit you every weekend and cut your grass."

"If you weren't a drug addict, you'd have more time for me."

"For the last time, I am not a drug addict!"

Ngin Ngin grinned her toothy grin. "I know. I tease."

Rebecca turned to Natalie. "We're having minestrone soup and tortellini for lunch."

"Rosetta helped me make tortellini," Ngin Ngin said. "Monday, I will teach her to make *doong*. Rebecca, you like to come? I can teach you, too."

"What about me?" Iris asked.

Ngin Ngin shook her head. "Won't let you in my kitchen again. Last time, you screwed up rice. How you managed, I don't know. There was a rice cooker! And Natalie will be back in Ottawa on Monday."

"Okay, I'll come," Rebecca said.

Rosetta stood up. "I should go now. I have plans with my son."

She hobbled to the door, and a few minutes later, Natalie, Rebecca, Iris, and Ngin Ngin were sitting at the table with bowls of minestrone. It was very different from the food Ngin Ngin usually cooked, but just as delicious.

"We made a big pot," Ngin Ngin said. "I will send leftovers home with Iris, since you cannot cook, and Rebecca, since you need lots of time to make a baby."

"Ngin Ngin!" Rebecca said.

"What? I want a great-grandchild. But am no spring chicken. Don't have all the time in the world."

"At Rebecca's wedding," Iris said, "you claimed you were as healthy as an ox and would live for a long time."

"Yes, that's what I hope. But you never know. Many things could happen. I will teach Rebecca to make *doong* so at least someone can make them when I'm gone."

Rebecca reached across the table and squeezed her grandmother's hand.

"I thought I would have great-grandchildren by now," Ngin Ngin said, "since Natalie is already way past thirty. Natalie, why don't you have children?"

Natalie didn't feel up to this. After the conversation with her sister last night, then her mother this morning, she'd prefer to talk about movies or TV or something like that. But she would be perfectly honest.

"Is the problem that you cannot find a man?" Ngin Ngin asked. "Why is that so hard? You very picky?"

"I don't want children," Natalie said. "Not everyone wants children. I don't need to have them."

Ngin Ngin frowned. "But you like babies, no?"

Natalie nodded. "I just don't want any of my own."

God, she'd been explaining herself over and over lately.

Ngin Ngin used her Chinese soup spoon to scoop up some minestrone. "In my day, everyone was expected to have kids, but now…I guess you have big important job. Don't understand it, but I think it is important? You trying to save the world?"

"Something like that."

"Do you really think we'll be able to?" Iris asked.

Natalie opened her mouth to respond, but Rebecca beat her to it.

"If Natalie was totally pessimistic," Rebecca said, "she wouldn't bother. She wouldn't take trains everywhere. She wouldn't eat meat only two or three times a week and live in a small condo so it takes less energy to heat."

"What is this word 'pessimistic'?" Ngin Ngin asked.

"It means you think the worst will happen," Natalie replied. Anthony had called her that, and it was a word she often used to describe herself, but Rebecca was right: Natalie did possess a shred of hope that humankind could figure out its problems, otherwise she wouldn't do many of the things she did.

"Is this why you don't want children? You think you would be a terrible mother?"

"No, no. It's nothing like that. I actually think I'd be a decent mother, but I wouldn't be a *great* mother because I never wanted kids in the first place. I would resent them."

They were quiet for a minute.

"I guess I understand," Ngin Ngin said at last. "It's okay, Natalie. Rebecca will make the babies. Simon called yesterday to say they will adopt a baby, too, or maybe it will be a small child, not baby anymore. I wish they lived in Toronto. Then I would visit all the time and drive them crazy. Lots of fun. Make them tortellini, too." She grinned. "I should get it now." She started to stand up.

"No." Iris jumped up. "Let me do it."

"I said before, I do not trust you in my kitchen."

"It's just dishing out food! That's not hard."

"Fine, fine. You better not screw up. Get chopsticks for everyone."

Iris headed to the kitchen.

"There are some people who don't have kids," Ngin Ngin said. "Like your uncle. Dennis, I think? The one kicked out of Seth and Simon's wedding?"

Natalie couldn't say she enjoyed being compared to Uncle Dennis.

"Except Uncle Dennis is a terrible person," Rebecca said, "and Natalie is not." She patted Natalie's hand. "There are lots of decent and caring people, not just our bigoted uncle, who choose not to have kids."

Natalie froze, her spoon halfway to her mouth.

Rebecca had stated such an obvious fact, and yet it was something Natalie had really needed to hear, especially from someone who meant a lot to her. Although she'd long been confident in her decision not to reproduce, she realized now that she'd still judged herself for that decision and felt less worthy because of it.

Including less worthy of love.

She'd internalized some of those judgments about child-free people being awful and selfish, which was easy to do because the person in her family who didn't have children was not the greatest human being. And dealing with this was probably more difficult for her than it was for Connor, since women were expected to have maternal instincts. People had certain expectations of women that they didn't have of men, at least not to the same degree.

So, despite her confidence in her decision, she'd still felt like a lesser person. But all of that had been buried deep within her. She hadn't realized that she'd believed so much bullshit until now.

You deserve it, Rebecca had said yesterday.

Her little sister was smart.

You're okay. I'm proud of you, Mom had said.

Natalie needed to listen to the women in her family. What she'd thought was too good to be true might actually be within her grasp.

She had to stop thinking Connor was too good for her. Yes, he was a good person, but so was she, and if he wanted to be with her, she could be with him.

She'd assumed their relationship was doomed because of all her unsuccessful relationships in the past twenty years, but that just meant she hadn't found the right guy. It only took one. Plus, many of those men had been assholes, and that did not describe Connor Douglas, not at all—she wouldn't have remained friends with him for so long if that were the case. And unlike the men she'd dated before, he wanted the same thing as her.

Connor was special, and she now believed they could make it work, believed this could truly be different. She didn't need to be held back by her past, or what had happened to her parents—she was her own person. Besides, there were many happy long-term relationships, including in her own family; she'd been focusing only on the negative.

Connor loved her…and she loved him. Yes, that was a recent development, but they'd known each other for many years. He knew exactly who she was, and despite that, he loved her. *Because* of that, he loved her.

They could be together after all.

Iris returned to the dining room with two plates of tortellini, which she set in front of Ngin Ngin and Natalie. Natalie picked up her chopsticks with shaking hands and popped a piece of tortellini in her mouth. "This is tasty."

"Lots of work to make it," Ngin Ngin said. "Do not expect tortellini every time you visit."

"All of your cooking is good, Ngin Ngin."

"I know."

"You're so humble," Iris said, returning to the kitchen.

"I know this word," Ngin Ngin said. "I do not see the point in being humble anymore. I am awesome!"

Natalie laughed.

"What about me?" Iris asked as she brought out the last two plates of pasta.

"You're awesome, too. You put up with me for the drive to Mosquito Bay, and for two nights at bed and breakfast. But you are not awesome in the kitchen."

"And I have a drug problem."

"I told you that was a joke!" Ngin Ngin turned to Natalie. "I will not tease you about babies anymore, but what about boyfriends? I can tease you about boyfriends?"

"You should tease her about Connor." Rebecca winked at Natalie.

"Very confused about Connor," Ngin Ngin said, picking up a piece of tortellini with her chopsticks. "I thought he was your boyfriend, then you said he was just a friend, then you stayed overnight in his room at bed and breakfast. Cannot keep track. What happened now?"

"He asked me out, and I turned him down."

"You don't want a baby, and you don't want a man, either? You like women instead?"

"I like men," Natalie said. "I like Connor…a lot. But I screwed up."

"Aiyah!" Ngin Ngin said. "Silly girl."

"I know. I'll fix it. Actually…." Natalie took out her phone and flipped to the Toronto-Ottawa train schedule. There was a train in a couple of hours.

Yes. She would go back tonight.

Actually, now she remembered that Connor was looking after Ariana this weekend, and she was supposed to help him. But she'd forgotten, and he hadn't reminded her. Maybe he'd decided he would rather not see her after she'd broken his heart last weekend.

Well, she would see him tonight and make things right.

Natalie started eating her tortellini in a hurry. "Rebecca, we need to go back to your place as soon as we finish here," she said between bites. "I'll get my suitcase and head straight to Union Station."

"Ah," Ngin Ngin said. "I understand. You are making big romantic gesture, like in movies! What will be your gesture?"

"I don't know," Natalie said, feeling frustrated. "Isn't it enough that I show up?"

"Men like when you cook for them. Unless you're Iris. I don't think even hungry man would like Iris's cooking."

"Ngin Ngin!" Iris said. "It's really not that bad. Last week I made…well, let's not talk about that. But at least I know how to boil water!"

Ngin Ngin frowned. "There are women who cannot boil

water? Really? That is sad. Even men should know how to boil water."

Rebecca squeezed Natalie's arm. "You have a long train ride to think about what you'll do when you see Connor. But you're right. The most important thing is that you're there. We'll leave in five minutes."

Ngin Ngin got up and shuffled to the kitchen. "I will get you dessert. Rosetta brought cannoli from the bakery near her house. You eat some now, then you bring some to your man, yes?" She came back with a small empty container and a larger container full of cannoli. Natalie reached for a cannoli and crammed it into her mouth. Normally, she'd eat it slowly and savor it, but now she could only think of Connor.

She remembered dancing together by the water in Mosquito Bay. Their first kiss. Meeting him for the first time, so many years ago. So many, many years before she figured out what he could mean to her.

But she didn't think of it as wasted time. She saw everything that had happened in the intervening years as necessary to get them to this point.

Maybe she could have accepted his feelings for her a week earlier if she hadn't run into Anthony pushing a stroller, if her own feelings of unworthiness hadn't been brought to the surface, but at least she'd figured it out eventually.

Ngin Ngin started filling the empty container with cannoli. "Need to find a man for Iris. Rosetta has a grandson. Maybe we set you up?"

"That's quite alright," Iris said. "I don't need my grandmother to play matchmaker. I'd prefer to keep my dating life separate from my family, thank you very much."

"Hmph. Well, you're still young. But in two years, if you have no man, I will get to work, yes? Might be difficult because you do drugs and can't cook, but I will manage. I will say you're very good at cutting my grass. Also, very friendly and charming and pretty. That should be enough." Ngin Ngin's eyes lit up. "I know! I will find a man who is a chef. He can cook for you and your children." She hesitated. "Unless you're like Natalie and don't want children? If so, it's okay."

"Can we not talk about this? I'm only twenty-six, and I'm not ready to think about kids. Right now, I just want to go home and do some drugs and forget about this conversation."

"Iris!"

"I'm joking, Ngin Ngin."

"You know Rosetta and I signed up for a cooking class in the summer? It is Thai cooking at the community center. Her grandson really likes Thai food, so she wants to learn. Maybe you could take the class with us, Iris? There might be a nice young man to rescue you when you set fire to kitchen."

Iris just covered her face and shook her head.

As entertaining as this was, Natalie had better go if she wanted to make that train. She stood up and grabbed the small container of cannoli. "Thank you for lunch. It was lovely."

"Glad you liked it," Ngin Ngin said. "You will come back and visit me soon, I hope. Bring Connor and I will make something special for him. Maybe I will know how to make pad Thai by then."

Natalie gave her grandmother a hug. "See you soon."

"Good luck with Connor!" Iris called out as Natalie and Rebecca headed to the door.

"Ah, soon it will be just you and me, Iris," Ngin Ngin said. "Maybe I can teach you how to make toast?"

Natalie loved her family, she really did. Even if weddings were always epic disasters.

Natalie tapped her fingers on the armrest, wishing the train would move faster. The trip from Toronto to Ottawa was several hours, but usually she didn't mind—she would read or do work. But now, she couldn't concentrate. She was thinking of Connor, and she hated that there were still so many kilometers between them.

Her phone rang. It was Simon.

"You have to settle a bet for us," he said.

Natalie sighed. "What is it this time?"

"Are you and Connor going out now?"

"Um. Not exactly."

"Define 'not exactly.'"

"He asked me out and I turned him down. But I've changed my mind, so I'm on my way to see him."

"Dammit," Simon said. "I guess that means Seth is technically correct. Why couldn't you have figured this out a day earlier?"

"What exactly was the bet?"

"I bet that you and Connor were now a couple. Seth bet that you would have fucked it up somehow."

"My brother has so much faith in me." She paused. "I wish I'd figured it out earlier, too, but some things take time." She'd needed to talk to three generations of women in her family to figure it out. "What did you lose?"

"We're having dim sum, and the pork buns and egg tarts come in plates of three. Now he gets the extra ones. You owe me."

"Fine. Next time I go to Vancouver, I will buy you that extra pork bun and egg tart."

"Bring Connor to Vancouver with you."

"I hope to," Natalie said. "I really do."

She ended the call and stared out the window. As the train rattled across the province, she realized that in the past several years, she had become even more prickly and cynical than before, and she hadn't let people get too close. She also realized that it had been a defense mechanism. A way of coping with the intrusive questions and comments she received, now that she was an unmarried, childless women in her mid-thirties. Plus, having her hopes crushed over and over had been emotionally exhausting, and so she'd put up walls around her heart. Had refused to let herself hope.

But now, she had lots of hope.

She would get Connor back.

[21]

Connor sighed when he heard tiny footsteps scamper down the stairs.

He'd put Ariana in his guest room, and she loved the queen-sized bed. *It's so big! Just like Mommy and Daddy's bed!* Last night, he'd carried out the bedtime routine that Mallory had given him, and Ariana had gone to bed at eight thirty and fallen asleep within minutes.

Tonight, however, was a different story.

It was nine thirty, and this was the third time Ariana had come downstairs. He turned down the volume on the hockey game as she approached.

"Uncle Connor." She frowned. "I'm scared. I think a really big monster could fit under the bed. Mommy says there's no such thing as monsters, but sometimes Mommy lies about things to make me feel better."

He suppressed a laugh. "There are no monsters under the bed. There's a special cleaning service that checks for monsters, and I had them come on Wednesday. They promise the house is free of monsters."

Ariana nodded solemnly. "I wish I had Beanie. He makes me

feel better, but I forgot him at home." Beanie was her beloved stuffed rabbit. There had already been one crying fit over his absence.

How did his sister do this every night?

Admittedly, Connor hadn't been himself for the past week. There was a heaviness to everything he did, and he knew exactly why that was.

"How about this," he said. "I'll come upstairs and lie on the bed with you for a bit. I'll turn on the lamp, and it'll be like your nightlight at home."

He turned off the TV, but before they could head upstairs, there was a knock at the door.

Ariana froze. "The monsters," she whispered. "They found me. Don't get it!"

"Somebody just has the wrong house. It's okay. They'll go away soon."

But then there was another knock, and his phone buzzed. He grabbed it off the coffee table.

I'm at your door, Natalie's text message said. *I know it's late, but I need to talk to you.*

His heart thumped in his chest. "It's a friend," he said to Ariana. "You can come to the door and meet her."

He opened the door, his niece clutching his leg.

Natalie was standing there with a small suitcase and a takeout bag. Her hair was a mess, and she was breathing a little heavily, as if she had run.

She was beautiful.

"Natalie," he said, "this is my niece, Ariana." He pulled her out from behind his leg.

Natalie bent down and held out her hand. Ariana shook it, her face serious.

"It's nice to meet you," Natalie said.

"I'm supposed to be in bed now, but I'm too scared to sleep and I miss Beanie. Uncle Connor is supposed to come upstairs and stay with me." Ariana looked at Natalie quizzically. "Are you Uncle Connor's girlfriend?"

"Something like that." Natalie looked up at him and smiled.

Last weekend, he'd declared his love for a woman for the first time in a very long time, and she'd turned him down.

But now she was in his front hall, and he couldn't help smiling stupidly at her. He knew why she was here.

"Let's get you to bed," he said to Ariana. He hoped she wouldn't come downstairs for yet a fourth time. He turned to Natalie. "I'll be back in a minute."

"Natalie should come upstairs, too," Ariana said. "If you lie on both sides of me, it will be harder for the monsters to get me."

He refrained from thinking about all the things he and Natalie could do in a bed.

A few minutes later, they were upstairs in the guest room, the lamp on the bedside table turned on low, Connor on Ariana's right side and Natalie on her left.

"Tomorrow, we're playing zookeeper," Ariana said to Natalie. "Uncle Connor will be the hippo. What do you want to be?"

"I could be a giraffe. My sister often wanted me to be a giraffe."

"Is your sister little like me?"

"No, she's all grown-up now."

"Does she still want you to be a giraffe?"

"Thankfully, no," Natalie said. "But I'll do it for you tomorrow, okay? Now close your eyes. You're safe here."

Connor was lying in bed with Natalie…and there was a child between them. This was not the future either of them wanted, but on a temporary basis, it was just fine. The important thing was that she was here.

It sounded like Ariana was asleep. He waited a few more minutes, then got up and headed downstairs. Natalie followed him to the couch in the living room.

"You came," he said, because that was all he could manage to say.

"I told you I'd help you babysit, didn't I?" She settled herself beside him.

"Natalie…"

She cupped his cheek in her hand. "I do want you very much, and I did last weekend, too. But I couldn't do it, not then. I had to realize something first, and that didn't happen until I went to Toronto to see Rebecca this weekend. I also talked to my mother and my grandmother." She paused. "The thing is, even though I was confident in my decision not to have children, I still felt like that made me a lesser person, less capable of love and less deserving of it."

It pained him to hear her say that.

"Of course," she continued, "I thought it was bullshit when people said that women who don't want children are shallow and self-absorbed. Still, I internalized it to some extent, in part because of Anthony. But I shouldn't have. I deserve this, and so do you. Yes, my parents' separation has rocked some of my faith in lasting love, and yes, I can be cranky and pessimistic, but despite all that, despite all of my unsuccessful relationships in the past, I still believe we can make this work—which says a lot about how I feel about you. I didn't think this would ever be possible for me, and then I found you. Or rather, I discovered I had feelings for you nearly two decades after meeting you for the first time."

When she'd shown up at his door, he'd known she wanted to be with him, but still, actually hearing these words fall from her lips nearly made the air whoosh out of him.

She grabbed the white plastic bag she'd set on the coffee table. "Do you remember the first dinner we ate together, back when we were students?"

He nodded. "We were studying for our first-term chemistry exam, and we left the library to get falafel sandwiches because your stomach was growling loudly. I had a crush on you back then, you know."

"You did?"

"I forced myself to get over it when you got a boyfriend, but now, it's different. Now, I'm not just an eighteen-year-old kid with a crush. You mean so much to me."

She smiled at him as she pulled a foil-wrapped package out of the bag. "Here. It's heavy on the pickles. I remember that's what you like, even though we haven't had falafels together since then."

"And yours has far too much tomato and olives."

She gave him a mock glare. "Not *too* much tomato and olives. Just the right amount, which is more than you put on, but that's because your tastes are not as refined as mine."

They both laughed quietly.

"Anyway," she said, "it's almost ten o'clock, and I'm sure you've already had dinner, but I haven't. I rushed to Ottawa from Ngin Ngin's house—as fast as one can rush on a train, that is. Unfortunately, we were stopped for half an hour near Kingston, and I was furious. I probably should have eaten on the train, but I was too anxious to see you and—"

"Natalie," he said, putting a finger to her lips. "Will you stop talking long enough for me to kiss you?"

He pulled her into his lap and slanted his mouth over hers. The moment his lips touched hers, he melted against her, joining in a way they never had before. He tightened his arms around her and pulled her as close as he could.

He never wanted her to leave.

"You'll stay the night, won't you?" he said. "We'll have to be quiet, but I think we can manage."

"Don't worry. I'm not going anywhere."

That was what he liked to hear. "If you ever doubt again that you can do this, or that you deserve it, I will make it my mission to prove to you otherwise. I wish people hadn't made you feel like crap for being who you are. I think you're perfect."

He kissed her again, until her stomach grumbled loudly. She laughed and picked up her falafel sandwich, but as soon as she took a bite, she made a face.

"Shit," she said. "I got them mixed up. This is the one with pickles. Disgusting." She handed it to him, then grabbed the other and took a bite. "Now *that* is good."

"What do you think would have happened if I'd kissed you all those years ago, when we were studying chemistry and eating falafels together?"

"I honestly don't know. I'm just happy we're together now, and my God, you are turning me into such a sap." She took a bite of her falafel sandwich. "Maybe I would have been disgusted because you tasted like pickles."

"Maybe you'll learn to like pickles."

"Not happening. There are some things that can't be changed, no matter how much we want them to, and that's okay. But other things…do change."

"How's Rebecca?" he asked. "Did you figure it out?"

She nodded.

"I'm glad."

"How has it been looking after Ariana?"

"I don't think I'm the greatest disciplinarian."

"You're the uncle. You're not supposed to be the disciplinarian."

He picked up a pickle that had fallen out of his pita. "It's been going okay for the most part. I just hope she stays asleep now."

Natalie put down her sandwich and snuggled against him. "Your sister will be okay with you introducing your girlfriend to Ariana?"

"Girlfriend," he repeated. "It's been a long time since I've had a girlfriend."

"Then let me update you on your duties as my boyfriend. Every morning, you must bring me breakfast in bed, including a generous amount of coffee. I expect very fine food, at least as good as the breakfasts at the bed and breakfast in Mosquito Bay. I also expect you to be fully nude and serenade me with your guitar as I eat."

"I don't play guitar."

"You can learn." She tipped her forehead against his. "You just need to be you. That's all I ask. I love you as you are."

His heart swelled at her words. "I love you, too," he murmured. "I hope you stay until Mallory comes to pick Ariana up tomorrow. She'll want to meet you."

"I met her at your wedding."

"Ten years ago," he said, "and under very different circumstances. I'm not sure she remembers you. It'll be good for you to get to know Mallory and Ariana, since I plan to keep you in my life for a long, long time."

"I sure hope so."

The next evening, Natalie sat down to a meal of pasta with mushroom sauce, green salad on the side. This was what Connor had intended to make for her last week, but she'd run out the door before he could start cooking, and now that Ariana had gone home with her parents, they could finally have their romantic candlelit dinner. They were sitting next to each other, Connor's hand on her thigh.

She was a little behind on this whole love business. Her younger brother had been married nearly ten years, and her much younger sister had tied the knot, too. But that was okay.

"Ngin Ngin made us tortellini yesterday," Natalie said. "She's friends with an Italian grandmother, who showed her how to make tortellini and minestrone. Ngin Ngin is going to teach her to make *doong*."

"What's that?" he asked.

"Sticky rice dumplings wrapped in bamboo leaves. She puts

pork and salted egg yolk inside. They're good. I hope you'll get to see my family again soon under more ideal circumstances. Something that doesn't involve a disastrous wedding."

"What do you want for your own wedding?"

Natalie nearly choked on her linguine, caught off-guard by the question.

"Someday. Not in the near future, but…someday." He raised his eyebrows.

"I never wanted a big wedding," she said, "and that's not only because I'm scared of the disasters that could occur, given my family history. But I would like a proper proposal, where you get down on one knee."

She nearly added, *I know that's kind of corny*, but she didn't. She wouldn't think of the things she wanted as lame and corny. She wanted a proposal, a nice small wedding, and no children, and there was nothing wrong with any of those things. Natalie could love herself just the way she was, and she believed that she deserved to have her dreams come true.

Connor kissed her on the cheek. "Then you shall have it. Someday."

Several minutes later, that kiss still lingered on her skin.

He took her upstairs and made love to her, and this time, there were no brother and brother-in-law in the room next door, nor was there a niece in the bedroom across the hall.

This time, she didn't have to worry about being too loud.

"Just you and me," he murmured. "Just you and me."

One year later...

THEY STOOD outside the entrance to the civic wedding chamber at Toronto City Hall. There were about thirty of them—mostly family, some friends.

It was Natalie's wedding day. At last.

Connor had proposed three months ago. He'd made her breakfast in bed on a random Saturday in March. She'd taken a sip of coffee and almost spit it out in surprise—yeah, she sure was classy—when she'd seen the ring on the tray, beside the orange juice. Then he'd gotten down on one knee and asked her to be his wife, and she'd cried as much as she had during *Moneyball*. He hadn't been naked, but that had happened shortly thereafter.

"Blue dress?" Ngin Ngin asked now. "Is this a new trend, wearing dresses that are not white for your wedding?"

Natalie shook her head. "No. Just something Rebecca and I did. According to Rebecca, this blue is *ocean dream*." That was the paint chip her sister had shown her the other day.

Rebecca stood beside her, wearing a maternity dress in a darker shade of blue. She was seven months pregnant, and

Mallory was just behind her at six months. Ariana would be getting a little brother soon, and she was looking forward to it. She wanted to name him Robin Hood.

Seth was chasing around his one-and-a-half-year-old daughter, whom they'd adopted three months ago. Natalie and Connor had met her for the first time when they'd gone out to Vancouver in April, and Natalie had bought Simon the pork bun and egg tart she'd owed him.

"Livvy," Seth called. "No pushing Ariana, okay?"

Livvy wandered over to Natalie, who picked her up.

"Pretty," Livvy said, poking Natalie in the boob.

"Aiyah!" Ngin Ngin cried. "She will get your dress dirty. Her hands have been everywhere. I can hold her instead. Am no spring chicken, but I can hold baby. Nobody cares if my dress is dirty."

She sat down on the bench and grinned when Natalie handed Livvy to her.

"She looks just like you, Simon," Ngin Ngin said.

"You do understand she's adopted, don't you?" Seth asked.

"Am not stupid just because I'm old. Was trying to make a joke. Why don't you like my jokes?"

By the window, Natalie's parents were having a polite conversation while Bernard stood silently beside her mother. He was a man of few words. Mom and Dad's divorce would be finalized soon, but they were still her parents, and they got along well enough when they had holidays together.

Grandma and Uncle Dennis weren't here. She hadn't invited them. Aunt Louisa was here, but now that she'd significantly cut back on her drinking, Natalie didn't expect her to make any inappropriate remarks.

Connor took Natalie's hand and squeezed it. "Don't worry. There's no dirt on your right boob." He dropped his voice. "But I promise to do a closer inspection later."

It wasn't all that funny, but she threw her head back and

laughed because she was just so happy. It was her wedding day, and she was surrounded by the family she loved, and, most importantly, the man she wanted to spend her life with.

Even if their wedding was a bit of a disaster, it would be okay as long as they were married. However, Natalie had planned for as simple a wedding as possible, and one of the benefits was that there were fewer things to go wrong. She'd completely axed wedding speeches, despite Rebecca's protests.

A couple emerged from the wedding chamber. Two women, both wearing white dresses and big smiles.

"Congratulations," Connor said as the newlyweds headed to the elevator.

He and Natalie made their way into the wedding chamber, followed by their families. Everyone took their seats, except the two of them. They walked down the very short aisle to the officiant, and Natalie looked up into Connor's eyes. She was filled with love, and gratitude that they had somehow made it to this moment.

"That was perfect," Natalie said after paying the bill at the Chinese restaurant where they'd had the reception. "As long as nobody starts puking tonight from food poisoning, it was perfect."

"It was," Connor said, leaning down to kiss her neck. "Now we can go back to the hotel, where no one in your family is staying."

That was the advantage of a late-morning wedding and an afternoon reception: she'd get to go to bed with her new husband well before midnight. They were spending two more nights in Toronto before they headed out to Newfoundland to go hiking in Gros Morne for their honeymoon.

The rain had held off for their pictures, but it was coming

down in sheets now. Natalie stepped outside anyway. It wasn't like she was planning to wear this dress again. The rain ruined her fancy updo, and water streamed down her chest and back. She threw her arms wide open, one hand carrying her bouquet of pink flowers.

"See?" Rebecca had said a few months ago. "Catching the bouquet at my wedding was good luck after all."

Natalie still thought that was a bunch of superstitious poppycock, but she'd smiled, glad that love was finally working out for her. She'd decided not to throw the bouquet at her own wedding; it was a silly tradition, plus she wanted to keep the bouquet for herself. She would dry the flowers, and it would be a keepsake of their special day.

It turned out that she was a little sentimental after all.

Now, she twirled around with her arms outstretched. She stopped spinning when Connor stepped toward her. He brought his mouth down on hers and kissed her in the rain.

"What about your tuxedo?" she asked, pulling back. "Your shoes?"

Instead of answering, he swept her up into his arms before setting his lips to hers again.

Afterward, they hurried to the hotel. As soon as they got inside their suite, they struggled with their soaking-wet formal clothes, tossing them on the ground so they could be skin against skin.

Cold, clammy skin against skin.

Maybe the rain was the "disaster" for her wedding day. It was for the best that it wasn't completely perfect—that would feel like bad luck. But she wouldn't complain about the rain at all, even if she was shivering now.

Connor rubbed his hands up and down her arms, and then he pulled her under the covers and did unspeakably dirty things to her.

Much, *much* later, she glanced at the clock.

"Wow," she said. "It's almost seven. What do you want for dinner? Lunch was pretty big, but I've worked up an appetite."

"I ordered something. It will arrive…actually, any minute now. I should get dressed."

He put on dry clothes: a pair of boxers, a T-shirt, and shorts. There was a knock at the door, and she watched his muscles ripple under the soft cotton as he moved to answer it.

A minute later, he returned with two falafel sandwiches, one with lots of pickles and one with lots of tomatoes and olives, as well as a bag of Cheetos. She eagerly reached for her sandwich and looked at the label.

"It's from the place where we ate together in first year," she said.

"It is. Almost twenty years later, and it's still in business."

"We're going to make a mess with those Cheetos."

He grabbed a set of chopsticks off the nearby table. "No, we're not."

"You certainly came prepared."

Connor opened the bag, picked up a single Cheeto with the chopsticks, and fed it to her.

It was the most sensual experience she'd ever had with Cheetos. Perhaps her husband should make a habit of feeding her Cheetos when she was naked in bed.

She took the chopsticks and used them to pluck a Cheeto out of the bag for him. When he smiled at her, his eyes crinkling, it hit her straight in the chest. This man was hers, and they would have a wonderful life together. Just the two of them.

The future she'd wanted but assumed would never happen…

Somehow, it was happening now.

ACKNOWLEDGMENTS

Thank you to Farah Heron, Ruby Lang, Rain Merton, and Suzanne Krohn for their help with the manuscript, and to my editor, Latoya C. Smith, for helping me make this book the best it could be. Thank you also to Toronto Romance Writers, as well as my husband and father, for all your support. And thank you to Flirtation Designs for the lovely cover!

Jackie Lau decided she wanted to be a writer when she was in grade two, sometime between writing "The Heart That Got Lost" and "The Land of Shapes." She later studied engineering and worked as a geophysicist before turning to writing romance novels. Jackie lives in Toronto with her husband, and despite living in Canada her whole life, she hates winter. When she's not writing, she enjoys gelato, gourmet donuts, cooking, hiking, and reading on the balcony when it's raining.

To learn more and sign up for her newsletter, visit jackielaubooks.com.

www.ingramcontent.com/pod-product-compliance
Lightning Source LLC
Chambersburg PA
CBHW021328190726
48288CB00003B/1014